Billy Blood

The Mason Braithwaite Paranormal
Mystery Series, book 4

In this series:

Signs Point to Yes

The Desert Rats

Reach for the Sky

Billy Blood

Rubber-Band Ball

The Invisible Arrow

Penstock Canyon

The Man from Grapalia

The Mythical Blond

Stealth Glasses

The Melted Pineapple

Night on the Water

The Landers Mystique

DAGMARMIURA.COM

Mason is a hero like none who have come before him: a sensitive, queer P.I. whose only weapon is his intuition. This book turns the detective genre on its head and makes you think about the ninety percent of your brain you're not using.
—Teja Watson, author of *Attic.doc*

Thanks to Christopher Church for giving us another exciting and well written adventure with one of my new heroes.
—Amos Lassen,
ReviewsbyAmosLassen.com

The paranormal aspect is subtle and stays within the realm of (maybe) possible. The point, though, is that Mason believes in it and follows his intuition through the twists and turns of the plot…. I'm so glad I started reading this series.
—Zoe E. Masongsong

The story has a fun and familiar aesthetic, as the characters sound like people I'd be friends with. The twists of the story are clever, and if you're anything like me, you will not see them coming. I really enjoyed this book!
—an Amazon customer

Billy Blood

Christopher Church

Published by Dagmar Miura
Los Angeles
www.dagmarmiura.com

Billy Blood

First published 2016

ISBN: 978-1-942267-16-4

Sunday

He saw it coming. A second or two before the crash the movement caught Mason's eye, approaching way too fast in the rearview mirror, a flash of dark blue, and then the impact. He had just enough time to lean back into the headrest and stomp down hard on the brake.

"Damn it," he said, after the sickening judder of the crash. He took a deep breath and made sure the car behind him wasn't still moving, then shifted the transmission into park. His heart was pounding from the rush of adrenaline. His propensity for this kind of mess was why Ned, his boyfriend, never let him drive his cars—luckily this one was a rental. And luckily he hadn't been pushed into the car ahead of him. He watched it pull slowly away in the stop-and-go traffic, then looked in the rearview mirror to see what the driver who hit him was going to do. They were in the second lane on a wide stretch of freeway, but the traffic on either side was moving slowly enough that it felt safe to get out. He sighed and pushed open the door, breathing deeply to calm himself down, hoping the other driver wouldn't be aggressive.

She stepped out at the same time Mason did—fortysomething, blond, dressed for an office job. She looked a little dazed, but that was understandable.

"Are you OK?" she called to him, concerned but not agitated.

"I'm fine," Mason said, raising his voice to be heard over the traffic.

"Are you sure? You look a little flushed."

"That's just because I'm a redhead," Mason said, running his fingers through his hair self-consciously. "What about you, are you OK?"

"Yeah." She closed her car door and walked to the front to assess the damage. "Watch the cars in the other lane," she said. She spoke with authority. Her tone reminded him of a cop he'd worked with recently on the gritty east side of LA County.

She was right about the traffic, he realized. It wasn't moving fast, but the cars coming up behind hers were jostling to merge into the other lanes, and one distracted driver could easily kill them both.

"I don't think this one can be driven," she said. It was a full-size sedan, but it must have slid under the back of the SUV Mason had rented, buckling the hood into an angry snarl and folding the grill in on itself. Mason's bumper was messed up, but it was definitely drivable. In the confusion he'd left it running, and the engine sounded fine.

"Do you want me to call the auto club?" he asked her. "I have my boyfriend's card."

"I'd appreciate that," she said, and nodded. "I'll get my insurance info."

He was grateful that she was so calm—it meant he could relax a little. She went back to her car and squeezed in the driver's door, keeping her eyes on the traffic. Mason pulled out his phone and stood flat against the back of the SUV to make the call, then went back to the driver's door to find his backpack, which held the rental contract.

It was so typical that something like this would happen to him the first time in months he climbed behind the wheel. Ned drove everywhere and never had any trouble; one trip to the thrift store to get a new desk and Mason was belly-up on the freeway.

"They'll be here soon," he told her, keeping close to the SUV to get back to her. "They said they have tow trucks out here at rush hour patrolling for things like this."

"This is a rental," she said, handing him a strip of printer paper that looked just like the one he had, "but this is all your insurance company should need."

"Mine too," Mason said, digging around in his backpack to retrieve his contract and then setting the bag against the SUV's rear tire. He handed her his paperwork, then pulled a dog-eared copy of his business card out of his pocket and passed that to her as well. "That's me," he explained.

"Psychic investigator," she said, glancing at the card. "I do love LA."

He guessed she was being facetious. He couldn't place her accent, which wasn't exactly Southern, or from the Northeast. Rather than engaging her thinly veiled skepticism, he pulled out his phone again and positioned her contract on the mangled sedan hood to photograph it. He didn't stop to read it, but looked at it long enough to see the name in the box for "renter": Catherine Reznik. It didn't seem to show her address, but there was a phone number with an area code he didn't recognize. She was definitely from out of town.

Catherine had her phone in hand too, but rather than photographing his contract, in his peripheral vision he saw her surreptitiously photograph him. He could understand why she'd do that, he thought, deciding not to question her about it; there was so much fraud involving insurance, it was probably a good idea to get photos of the driver. He wouldn't bother photographing her, though, because it was unequivocally her fault, and he'd bought as much insurance as the rental agency would sell him—he wouldn't need to prove anything.

She photographed his rental contract too and gave it back to him. "We'll let the insurance people figure it out, shall we?" she said. "That's what we pay them for."

"That suits me," Mason said.

"I'm going to unload my stuff so that they can just tow this mess away."

He watched from the relative safety of a spot beside the SUV's crumpled bumper as she pulled a black wheelie bag and a briefcase out of the sedan's trunk, glancing up frequently to check on the cars crawling by. From the passenger compartment she grabbed a canvas shoulder bag, then she piled it all on the pavement next to the SUV.

"If I can't ride in the tow truck, maybe you can give me a lift," she said.

"Of course," Mason said, surprised that she'd be so nervy. He saw the flickering orange lights of the tow truck pulling up behind Catherine's car.

Wisely, the driver parked the truck slightly into the left lane, creating a couple of feet of protected space beside the disabled vehicles.

"Having some trouble?" the driver asked cheerily as he climbed out and inspected the damage. He was a burly guy with grease-stained hands. After he'd looked things over he grinned broadly and said, "What a mess. Which one is yours, Stretch?"

It wasn't the first time Mason had heard that one; he towered over the guy, and was taller than most people he met. Someone had once told him tall guys came in two configurations: string bean and rugby. Mason was definitely the latter.

"The SUV's mine," he said.

"It looks like it's drivable," Catherine said, her tone businesslike, "but you'll have to tow the sedan."

"Are you sure?" the tow truck driver asked, crouching down on the pavement and looking under the front end. "It's not leaking fluids." He stood and pried up one side of the buckled hood. "Things still look intact in here. I'm wondering if the damage is just cosmetic. Can you try starting it?"

Catherine climbed in and turned the key; the engine sounded normal.

"Turn the steering wheel left and right," the driver said. She complied, and he said, "I think you can drive it, at least as far as a body shop. I'll follow you off the freeway in case it dies, but I think you're both good to go." He pointed to the luggage piled beside the SUV. "Is any of that hers?" he asked Mason.

"Most of it," Mason said, and retrieved his backpack.

"Pop the trunk," the driver called to Catherine, and carried her wheelie bag over.

Mason walked back to her car and leaned down as she lowered the window. "Are you going to be OK?"

She smiled at him. "I appreciate your concern. I'll be fine."

The tow truck driver had returned to the SUV, and crouched down to inspect beneath its bumper. "This one's fine—hardly a scratch," he called to them. "We'll let you go first, Red."

Mason climbed into the SUV and dropped

his backpack on the passenger seat. Taking a deep breath, he shifted into gear and gingerly massaged the accelerator with his foot, pulling away slowly. The ambient traffic speed had picked up, and he glanced in the rearview for a last look at Catherine and the tow truck before focusing on getting back to the car rental office. He had already delivered his desk. Now he just had to return the vehicle and explain the damage.

He got off the freeway and a few minutes later was parked at the rental office, glad to see his bicycle was still locked to a street sign on the busy boulevard out front. He went in and set the keys and his contract on the counter.

"Hi, Viviana," he said, reading the clerk's name-tag. "Someone rear-ended me on the freeway, so the car is a little banged up."

"Oh, yeah," she said, disinterested, and scanned the barcode on his contract. She studied her computer screen for a moment. "You seem to have doubled down on insurance, so all you'll need to do is fill out a form." She slid a document on a clipboard across to him, and then a pen.

"Chelo!" she shouted into the doorway behind her. "Order up—damage!"

Soon a young guy wearing the same corporate shirt as Viviana trotted out to inspect the SUV.

Mason spent a few minutes detailing the accident in writing, trying to remember exactly where it had happened, finally writing "on the 5, near the 2." He consulted his phone to get details from Catherine's rental contract and was signing the bottom when Chelo came in from the parking lot carrying a black briefcase and a canvas shoulder bag.

"Just the rear bumper," he said to the other clerk. To Mason, he said, "I'm sure you wouldn't want to leave your briefcase behind," and set the bags on the counter.

"That's not my stuff," Mason said.

Chelo's eyes narrowed. "It was in the backseat of the SUV you were driving."

"The tow truck driver must have put the other driver's stuff in my car," he said. "We were stopped in the middle of the freeway, and he assumed it was mine. I'm sure you can track her down through the insurance company."

"Dude," Chelo said. "It's nothing to do with us. If you want to get it back to her, that's on you." He walked away.

"That should do it," Viviana said with a perfunctory smile, then handed him a printed receipt and stepped away.

He looked at Catherine's stuff. It would be awkward to cycle home with it, and he could easily just walk out and leave it. She's the one who caused the accident—why should her losing track of her things become his problem? But he could phone her later, and have her drop by to pick it up, which really involved minimal effort on his part. Annoying as it was, he knew it was the right thing to do.

He pulled the bags off the counter and carried them out to his bike, rolling up the shoulder bag and strapping it and the briefcase to the rack over his back wheel. He looped the bungee cord around it, then saddled up and set off for home.

He and Ned and their roommate, Peggy, lived in a dense and hilly little Los Angeles neighborhood, and the end of any outing always had Mason panting and sweating as he rode up the hill to their house. He put his bike in the garage and took Catherine's bags inside, dropping them on the floor by the front door with his backpack as he went into the kitchen to rehydrate. One simple errand and the subsequent fender-bender had taken the better part of the day, and the late-afternoon sun was now streaming in the French doors.

He wanted to set up his desk, so he went down the hall to the office he shared with Ned. They both worked from home, and Ned had a decent home office set up, but Mason was pretty new at this, and had recently decided his rickety old college desk would no longer do. Earlier Ned had helped him carry in the one he'd found at a thrift store, but it wasn't positioned yet, and the contents of his old desk were still piled haphazardly around the floor. It all seemed overwhelming, so he went back to the living room and collapsed on the sofa, taking a few minutes to decompress.

Eventually his mind wandered to Catherine's briefcase and shoulder bag, sitting there by the door. He pulled out his phone and found the image of her rental contract, and dialed the number she had listed. It rang a couple of times and then stopped, as if someone had picked up, but no one spoke. "Hello?" Mason said. He heard a couple of clicks on the line, and a recording started: "The number you have reached is not in service...." He looked at the photo of the contract again and redialed, just to be sure, and this time the recording started before it even rang.

Great—now he was holding Catherine's stuff and had no way to contact her. He went to the front door and picked up her bags, along with his backpack, and took them over to the sofa. Maybe there was some other way to find her. He pulled his laptop out of his bag and fired it up, then searched online for the phone number; it wasn't listed anywhere, but the area code was in Maryland. With a little more digging he found that the prefix indicated it was a landline in a town called Severn. A search for her name turned up other people with that name in other states and abroad, but no one in Maryland. He pulled his yellow legal pad out of his backpack and found a pen. This was getting complicated enough that he wanted to keep the facts straight. He jotted down:

Catherine Reznik
phone number not in service
landline in Severn, MD

It wasn't a lot to go on. He picked up her briefcase and tried to open it, but it was locked, the little combination-lock wheels set on triple zeros. It was fairly heavy, so she was probably missing her computer, or at least a lot of paperwork. He pulled open the canvas bag and found a thick blue woolen sweater. More evidence that she was from out of town: springtime in Los Angeles had been warm and humid in recent weeks, rendering such a heavy garment useless. There was also a little white notepad, but nothing was written on it. It was the kind of thing hotels and pharmacists gave away: each sheet had an emblem in the lower right corner that he didn't recognize, in the shape of a shield, with the initials BHC inside it in dark blue. He held it up toward the window at an angle to see if there were any indentations in the paper, traces of something written and torn off, but the surface was smooth and new.

The most interesting item in the canvas bag was a folder emblazoned with the acid-yellow and blue logo of something called Billy Blood. He flipped it open and found a couple of slick full-color brochures, as well as a sheaf of black-and-white pages with columns of numbers and dense paragraphs of legalese. He scanned the marketing materials and soon learned what Billy Blood was: an energy drink laced with "the goodness of real goat's blood." As a vegan, he found it appalling, but there was more and more of this kind of thing appearing every day—along with the burgeoning economic might of East Asia, where any living thing could be considered dinner.

The folder didn't contain anything personal or anything linking it to Catherine, but it seemed official, which implied that she might work there. He did a Web search for Billy Blood and found that their head office was here in LA. Maybe Catherine was in town doing business with them.

He sighed and put the folder back in the bag, along with her sweater and the notepad. Maybe there was no connection at all. There was nothing he could do about it on a Sunday evening, though; he'd phone their offices tomorrow, and ask for her, and go from there.

Back in the office, he pushed and dragged his new desk until it seemed like it was in the right place, facing the door, with the chair back to the window. He loaded his paperwork and other office stuff into the drawers, and admired his new acquisition. It didn't take up that much real estate, which was a prerequisite, considering that Ned's fifties modernist monstrosity was hogging up most of the room. This thrift-store gem was a nice contrast, dating to the 1930s or 1940s, with just enough ornamentation in the dark wood to give it an elegant feel. He'd find a green-shaded banker's lamp, and it would be exactly the look he was going for—"psychic investigator," in no uncertain terms.

Before long, Ned and Peggy got home, each carrying grocery bags.

"Where were you two?" Mason asked, coming out of the office to greet them.

"Farmers market," Peggy explained. During the week she worked for stodgy lawyers and had to look the part, but today she was dressed for a day off, in jeans and a billowy top, her long brown hair tied loosely behind her head.

"Artichokes are in season," Ned said. "How do you feel about artichokes with habanero aioli?"

"Oh, yeah, definitely," Mason said, giving him a powerful hug, then looking into his eyes and running his fingers through Ned's thick dark hair. Not as tall as Mason, he had dark Latin features. He always looked put-together and polished, even for a trip to the farmers market.

"What's this?" Ned said. "You're acting like you haven't seen me in weeks."

"I had a near-death experience today," Mason said.

Ned frowned. "Again? Come and tell me about it while we cook." He didn't seem overly worried, but it was true that Mason had been in several scrapes recently; perhaps Ned was getting inured to it.

"What happened?" Peggy asked him, looking more concerned. "Are you OK?"

"Just shaken up," he said.

"OK," she said, looking him over carefully. To Ned she said, "I'll prep the artichokes if you do the aioli?"

"Deal," he said, following her into the kitchen and slipping on an apron.

"Can I help?" Mason asked. In the years they'd lived together, Ned and Peggy had both made vegan cooking a pastime, and Mason ate well because of it. Sometimes he helped with food prep, but usually he got a pass.

"Nope," Ned said. "Tell us what happened."

Mason climbed onto a stool on the other side of the counter that separated the kitchen from the living room, and told them the whole story.

Ned put the aioli in a bowl and had Mason set it on the dining table. Peggy brought over three freshly steamed artichokes and a cold chickpea salad, and they sat down to eat.

"I never drive," Mason said, "and the first time I get behind the wheel, *bam*."

"It's all random chance," Ned said, pulling leaves from his artichoke. "It can happen to anyone. The good news is that no one got hurt. And it wasn't your fault—you can just walk away."

"Not quite—I wound up with the woman's briefcase." He explained how that had happened, and told them about finding the Billy Blood folder.

"What's Billy Blood?" Peggy asked.

"Not while we're eating," Mason said. After they'd finished, he brought the folder to the table. "They put real goat's blood in the drink," he explained. "The idea came from China."

"Ew," Peggy said, pulling out the marketing brochures.

Ned flipped through the rest, studying the pages.

"This is a prospectus," he said finally.

"Which is—what?" Mason asked. Ned worked with bankers on something to do with mortgages that Mason had never clearly understood, but it meant he had a firm grasp on financial matters.

"They're trying to sell shares in the company, and this is the marketing material to convince people to buy in. It says they had their IPO last week."

"OK, I'm starting to feel stupid. What's an IPO?"

"It's when a company starts to sell shares on the stock market. It's usually a way to expand the company quickly, because they take in a lot of cash."

"That sounds like bad news for the goats of the world," Peggy said. "This stuff should be illegal."

"It also doesn't really help me figure out if this woman is connected to the company," Mason said.

"There's definitely a connection, if she was carrying this around," Peggy said.

"You should call them," Ned said. "Maybe someone there will know her."

Mason cleaned up after dinner, letting Ned relax. Peggy was playing a gig at a pub later on, and she spent an hour getting ready. Her stage persona, Peggy Pregnant, struck a memorable visual: an extremely pregnant folk singer dressed for the 1960s, complete with bell-bottom jeans and a daisy-spangled headband over her long hair. She had worn the strap-on fake belly in her performances for years, and no one had ever asked why she hadn't had the baby yet.

Mason spent some time at his new desk, and

waved good-bye to Peggy as she maneuvered her massive baby bump and her guitar case past the office door. Eventually he realized he was tired. Ned was already in bed, reading, when he climbed in.

"So you're not too shaken up?" Ned asked, setting his book aside and snuggling up to Mason.

"I'm glad I don't have to get back into a car any time soon," he said. "I was even a bit nervous on my bike. It feels like when there's an earthquake— everything seems fragile and unstable for a while after."

"I get that," Ned said, nuzzling Mason's arm. "Things will look different in the morning."

One of the techniques Mason used to get psychic insight was lucid dreaming—becoming aware of a dream and manipulating it. He told himself to dream about Catherine, to find some way to contact her, and gave himself the suggestion: wake up inside the dream.

Later, he was in an alley, at night, dimly lit, surrounded by concrete and brick. He walked up to a steel door and knocked on it. A speakeasy hatch in the door slid open, and a voice said, "Who're you?"

Mason knew he was dreaming, and managed to take charge of the dream, and maintain focus so that it didn't destabilize. "It's me," he said. "Open up."

"You can't," the voice said, and the hatch began to close.

"Wait," Mason said. "Why not? Explain yourself."

The sliding hatch paused, still partway open.

"Information only goes one way: in, not out."

"OK, well, you just gave me some information, so you're breaking your own rule."

With that the dream destabilized, and the scene tumbled into chaotic shapes and colors. Mason forced himself to wake up, and scrabbled for the pen and notepad he kept in the nightstand drawer. "Speakeasy," he wrote. "Information in—not out."

Monday

Mason hadn't set an alarm, as he didn't have any work to do. He got out of bed when his body told him to and headed down the hall to the kitchen, poking his head into the office on the way.

"Good morning," he said to Ned, who was engrossed in his computer screen. "Want some breakfast?"

Ned looked at his watch. "Technically it is still morning," he said, "but I had breakfast three hours ago. I'll have lunch with you, though."

Ned made a sandwich while Mason got the espresso machine running, pouring the entire little pot into a coffee mug. After some fruit and oatmeal and another pot of espresso, Mason started to feel awake, and followed Ned into the office, pulling open his laptop. It took a lot of effort just to find a phone number for the Billy Blood Corporation, but eventually he did. He dialed it and spent ten minutes navigating a tortuous labyrinth of recordings, finally giving up in frustration.

"Can you believe you can't leave a voice mail for a human being anywhere in their phone system?" he asked Ned.

"Sure can," Ned said, looking up from his computer screen. "Lots of companies are ditching voice mail altogether. If you're lucky, they might let you send an email."

"That's not going to work. I'll never hear back from them."

"Didn't you say their offices were here in town?"

"Yeah, on Sunset," Mason said, and read him the street address he'd found.

"That's on that bougie part of Sunset, by the comic-book store. Why not just go over there?"

It was a good idea, Mason realized. He folded his laptop shut and pulled his backpack on, kissed Ned good-bye, and carried Catherine's bags out to the garage. He strapped them on his rear rack and headed out, coasting down the hill toward the boulevard, the invigorating noonday sun lifting his spirits, spurring him to pedal faster.

He pulled up in front of the office, a stylish glass-and-concrete structure that predated the existence of the current corporate tenant by a few decades. This western side of Hollywood had always been home to upscale white-collar film industry or industry-adjacent offices; he tried to remember what had been there before the acid-yellow Billy Blood logo, but couldn't.

Locking his bicycle to a parking sign, he unstrapped Catherine's gear, pulling the canvas bag over one shoulder and carrying the briefcase. With any luck he wouldn't have to bring it back out. After a set of shallow stairs, he entered the lobby and found a reception desk, with the garish product logo dominating the wall behind it. A young woman in a tight dress smiled at him as he walked up.

"Can I help you?" she asked.

"I'm looking for someone by the name of Catherine Reznik," he said, and pulled the prospectus out of the shoulder bag.

"Let me get Mr. Davis," she said quickly, eyeing the folder. "He'll be able to help you. May I take your name?"

Mason recited it and watched her write it phonetically on a sticky note. He stepped back to look around the lobby while he waited. Considerable expense had gone into creating a stylish and modern vibe, with dark red-stained wood, frosted glass, and a couple of strategically placed Barcelona chairs.

"Mr. Braithwaite," a voice boomed from the elevator lobby.

"Mr. Davis," Mason said.

"Guilty," he said, too loudly, a broad smile on his face.

Mason knew this guy, even though they'd never met; the cut of the suit, the trendy haircut, even the absurdly white teeth—everything about him screamed sales. He shook Mason's hand vigorously and then cupped his shoulder, steering him toward the elevators. "Let's go upstairs, shall we?"

Mason followed him into an elevator car, but said, "I'm really just looking for someone—"

"Of course, of course. We can answer any questions you have," Davis said, and punched the button for the third floor as the doors slid closed. "Did you enjoy the IPO presentation? It was a shame about the storms that day. I don't think I could live in New York, you know? It's always either raining or it's a hundred degrees."

"I wasn't there," Mason said.

"I understand," Davis said, nodding confidently, and led Mason out of the elevator to an empty conference room across the hall.

"I really just wanted to ask about someone named Catherine Reznik."

"If you'll give me a moment," Davis said, "I'll fetch Mr. Frey. He'll be glad to meet with you."

Before Mason could protest, he was gone. The slick bastard, he thought, irritated. They were always like that—great at talking a big game but not willing to listen. Mason had once been submerged in the corporate world, and even though it felt like a different lifetime, being reexposed to it quickly evoked his ire.

He pulled out one of the plush chairs and sat, setting Catherine's bags in front of him on the vast table. Frey. That name was familiar—where had he seen it?

"Mr. Braithwaite," Davis roared again, entering the room, "this is Tyler Frey, our CEO."

Mason rose and greeted him. Frey had a broad, empty smile on his face, and looked more like a surfer than a CEO, with tousled blond hair and a deep tan, but he wore a sharp suit like Davis's, and a flashy watch. Davis left but didn't close the door, and Frey sat near Mason, at the end of the conference table.

"Call me Tyler," Frey said. "Everyone does. So Davis said you weren't at the IPO event in New York, but you were one of the West Coast invitees?"

Finally it clicked—they thought he was an investor. "I wondered why I was getting the VIP treatment," Mason said, and picked up the prospectus. "I wasn't invited to anything. I'm here because someone left this in my car."

"I see," Frey said, the sparkle leaving his eyes.

"Sorry to disappoint you," Mason said. "A woman named Catherine Reznik left this in my car, and I thought maybe she worked here."

"I've never heard that name before. We only have nineteen employees, so I'm certain she's not involved with the company."

"She had this, though," Mason said, waving the prospectus. "Could you find her in your records?"

Frey shook his head. "She would have picked that up at the IPO. But it was an open event—there were hundreds of people there, and we don't have records of their names." He sat forward in his chair, preparing to rise. "She might work for a bank or a brokerage, if that helps."

"Not really," Mason said, and looked at the briefcase. "I should have realized she wasn't the Billy Blood type."

"And what type is that?" Frey said, pausing in his chair, a faint smile on his lips.

"Well, I assume your market is Chinese, isn't it? She's Anglo, from Maryland."

"Some of our client base is Chinese, yes, but it's a product with very wide appeal. Have you tried it?"

"Hell, no. I'm vegan."

"Oh, one of those," Frey said, his face clouding. "We've had trouble with you people."

"I can understand why. The whole idea is morally bankrupt," Mason said.

Frey's eyebrows shot up. He probably wasn't used to having his beloved product critiqued to his face, Mason realized.

"So you're above profiting from anything you don't agree with? What do you do for a living, Mr. Braithwaite?"

"I never said I was above anything," Mason said, feeling the color rise in his cheeks. "I just don't like the idea of drinking blood." He added, "I work as a psychic."

"Seriously?" Frey said, his pique shifting to curiosity. "What kind of psychic?"

"Research and investigations. Missing people, stolen property, that kind of thing. I don't talk to the dead—some psychics do, but not me. And I don't do boy-girl stuff, ferreting out infidelity."

"Do you have a business card?"

Mason fished in his pants pocket and pulled one out, sliding it along the table to him.

Frey studied it for a moment and then looked up at him. "People actually pay you?"

"Not enough to be a venture capitalist, but I make a living."

"Tell me something psychic."

Mason didn't like Frey's slick veneer, and resented being challenged so blatantly. But before he could even formulate a response, an image popped into his mind: a person wearing a hood, or a cowl, taking off a robe, and then another robe, and below that another, layered like an onion. He couldn't tell who it was, but he knew the message was more about the image than it was about identity. It felt like a valid psychic insight, and it had appeared at the moment the guy had asked for it. Surely he had to tell him about it, even if presenting it on demand felt like a cheap parlor trick.

"You're a private person," Mason said, trying to interpret what he'd seen. "Lots of secrets." It was a milder spin on what he thought it really meant—that Frey engaged in layers of deception, some of them darker than others.

Frey laughed. "True," he said, "but that seems a little easy. Lots of people fit that description. Tell me something profound."

His attitude was infuriating, but Mason bristled at the challenge. He thought for a moment, then threw out an idea that wasn't specifically about Frey. "How about this: eternity is all around you, all the time."

Frey considered that, and then said, "That sounds kind of weighty, but what am I supposed to do with it?"

"Exactly," Mason said. "That's the whole point. It's a profound truth, but I doubt you'd be able to find a way to monetize it, so it's essentially useless to you."

Frey stared at him. "You don't think much of me, do you," he said.

"It's not personal," Mason said. "It's the whole corporate thing, selling things that people don't need."

"You do understand what money is, though, don't you?" Frey said, his voice rising. "That it's valuable, and desirable?"

"Sure. But there are lots of ways to make money."

Frey threw his head back and laughed. Mason wasn't sure why; he wasn't trying to be funny. He eyed the briefcase on the table. It was time to extricate himself.

"I love the idea of a psychic. It snags your attention," Frey said. "Just that word." He sat watching Mason, a thoughtful look on his face.

Mason sat forward. "I won't waste any more of your time."

"Hang on," Frey said, and held up a palm. "You're an investigator, right? Maybe I have a job for you."

"I appreciate that," Mason said slowly, "but I don't think I could work for you—the animal blood and all that."

"I'm not going to make you slaughter the goats," Frey snapped. "Do you know how many animals die from the pesticides used to produce your tofu and brown rice? It's all nuance, Mr. Braithwaite, not black and white."

"I get that," Mason said. He knew the guy had a point; it was impossible to disconnect completely from something as ubiquitous as animal exploitation. "And you should just call me Mason. What kind of job are you talking about?"

"Good." Frey smiled. "One of your people—the vegans—has been defacing our billboards and even the product on store shelves. I'd like you to look into that."

"Vandalism? That's a criminal thing. You should call the cops."

"They have bigger fish to fry than someone dabbing paint on a billboard." He shook his head. "No, we have to do this in-house. I love the idea of doing it psychically. If you can figure out who's behind it, then we'll call the cops."

"What did the vandals do, exactly?"

"They painted 'Leave the goats alone' on several

billboards around town. There have also been incidents in liquor stores where the same message was painted on cans of Billy Blood."

"And no one took credit?"

"No." His eyes narrowed. "It's just terrorism."

Mason frowned. "It doesn't sound like it merits that label. Have they done anything violent?"

"Not yet. But we just had our IPO, so we'll be moving into other markets around the country with advertising and product, and we need to get a handle on this. The expansion is going to happen quickly—the IPO raised 1.3 billion."

"Wait," Mason said. "Billion, with a 'b'? Dollars?"

"Yes. Wall Street sees great potential in our product."

"But you said you only have nineteen employees."

"The product is manufactured by subcontractors in China, so that's where the labor is concentrated. They can it there for the Asian market, but for the U.S. it's shipped over in tanks and canned by another subcontractor right here in town." He leaned forward and grinned conspiratorially. "The markup on a can of Billy Blood is, like, four thousand percent. It's a license to print money."

Mason nodded. He wanted more details before he could commit to the job, but at least he knew Frey could afford to pay him.

"So when did this happen?" Mason asked. "Was it one day, or a series of incidents? When and where was the most recent attack?"

"I'll give you a copy of the case file, with all the details, if you decide you want to take the job," Frey said. "But first, tell me about your methodologies."

"I usually start with psychometry, which is a way to read latent information from metal objects. In this case, maybe I could look at the stuff that got vandalized. I can also get insight from going to a place, like where it happened, and sometimes from interviewing people." He didn't mention lucid dreaming—it would sound passive, even lazy, and a dedicated capitalist would better understand the more active methods.

"That sounds reasonable," Frey said. "What are your rates?"

"A grand per day, plus expenses," Mason said. He would never quote so high for a regular job, but this guy had just told him he was worth over a billion dollars.

"That works," Frey said, not even hesitating. "Do you think you could wrap it up in a week?"

"I can try," Mason said, even though he had no idea what the work was going to entail.

"A written report from you, then, a week from today. I'll pay you half your base rate for the week when you get started, half on delivery. How does that sound?"

"Great."

"You'll have to sign a nondisclosure agreement, of course, and some other paperwork. Now that we're publicly traded, everything has to go by the book. Let me get the file," he said, and walked out.

Mason swiveled his chair around to look out the windows. The conference room wasn't high enough to have a grand vista, but even from the third floor there was a sweeping view of the basin, concrete and palm trees and haze stretching off toward Long Beach. He hadn't expected to find work today, much less from a sugary drink huckster. Was he betraying his own values by working for the guy? The thought made him uneasy. It was startling that there was so much freaking money in a business like this, in a product he'd never heard of. There was so much more going on in this massive city than he'd ever be able to fathom.

Frey came back in and slid a manila folder across to him. "Have a look," he said.

It was pretty thin, just a few sheets of paper with a list of the dates and locations of the vandalism, and a series of photos of the damage. "Leave the goats alone" had been painted in pink over the Billy Blood logo on a billboard, and messily stenciled onto a display of cans on a store shelf. Below that was a copy of a newspaper article, dated a week earlier, from the *Charlotte Scoop & Analyzer.*

"That's one of the papers that the Wall Street players read," Frey said, "even though it's from the South. That story put the word out that Billy Blood is relevant. It lined up nicely with the IPO."

Mason knew that any media coverage was a good thing for sales, but he was still shocked that Frey seemed almost proud of this. He looked back to the article. The headline read "Soft Drink Targeted in Terror Attack." There was that word again.

"Isn't 'terror' kind of an exaggeration?" Mason asked.

"Not at all. Just because they haven't gone violent yet doesn't mean they won't. Whoever's doing this is crazy, and they're targeting my company."

"OK, but I doubt that this is technically terrorism," Mason said.

"Do you see the list of shops in there?" Frey said impatiently, clearly done discussing semantics. "I'll have one of my people set you up with one of them tomorrow. You can do an interview and get started. How does that sound?"

"I guess that's a reasonable starting point."

Frey rose, followed by Mason. He pulled open his backpack and slid the manila folder inside. He'd almost forgotten about Catherine's bags, sitting there, inscrutable, still his responsibility. He stuffed the prospectus back into her shoulder bag.

"I'll take you to our staffing person," Frey said, and led him to the elevator.

"So is the vandalism happening in China too? The file only mentioned LA."

"No—they don't tolerate dissent over there. Deface a billboard and you get sent to a labor camp. They are good consumers, though—they're drinking Billy Blood like it was water." As they stepped into the elevator, he punched the button for the second floor and said, "You mentioned expenses, but we didn't clarify that. What possible expenses could you have? Windex for your crystal ball?"

"Funny," Mason said, his cheeks reddening. "It's just in case anything comes up. Sam Spade always asked for expenses, so I thought I should too."

"Excellent logic," Frey said. He looked thoughtful for a second, and added, "I'm giving a talk about the product here on Wednesday. You should come. There'll be food and booze."

"That sounds like fun," Mason hedged.

"I'll have one of my people send you the details."

The elevator opened and Mason followed Frey to a small office where a harried-looking woman sat surrounded by stacks of paper.

"Mason, this is Ms. Weston," Frey said. "I've put Mason on a week's contract." He explained what he wanted her to do.

"Of course," she replied deferentially.

"I'll leave you to it, then," he said, and to Mason, "We'll be in touch. Call me if anything comes up."

"I can't," Mason said. "No one at your company answers the phone."

"Right," Frey said, and fished a business card out of his breast pocket. "That's my direct number."

Weston relaxed visibly when he'd left, and started digging through her piles of paper.

"You do payroll?" Mason asked her.

"No. I'm a lawyer," she said tersely, but didn't elaborate. She handed him a thick document. "This is the nondisclosure agreement, and I'll find the tax form."

It was twelve pages long and written in legalese, but he knew he had to read through it, at least to get the gist of what he was agreeing to. Most of it seemed logical, forbidding him from sharing trade secrets. One section was less straightforward, and seemed to imply that the company owned all video and images they created of Mason.

"Is someone going to photograph me?" he asked Weston.

"It's a standard form," she said impatiently. "It covers every potentiality. Just sign it. It'll be fine."

Interesting advice from a lawyer, he thought, but he scanned the last few paragraphs quickly, then signed. Weston pulled it back and slid a tax form in front of him.

"Just to be clear, nondisclosure means you can't talk about the company outside the company," she said as he filled in the boxes.

"Got it," Mason said, glancing up at her, although he couldn't imagine that the intent of the contract was so strict.

Ten minutes later he was strapping Catherine's bags onto his bicycle again. He set off for home, riding on back streets and enjoying the sunshine and the warm spring air. He was glad to have found some work without even trying, even though the product was so obnoxious. He felt that fleeting uneasiness again, wondering whether working for Frey made Mason responsible in some way for something he found so reprehensible. The psychic image he'd picked up about the guy was dark, and implied that he couldn't be trusted. Hopefully that wouldn't impact the work.

After he'd pedaled up the hill and parked his bike, he brought Catherine's stuff into the house, and wondered where to put it. It didn't seem right to stick it in a closet to be forgotten, but he didn't want to be tripping over it either. Ned and Peggy were both out, and he stood there in the silent house, considering it. Finally he set the bags beside his desk, so he'd be reminded to work on finding her. For now, though, he had a paying gig.

He read through the file Frey had given him, but it was really just an accounting of the vandalism. The article from the *Scoop & Analyzer* didn't include anything beyond that, talking instead about the upcoming IPO. He labeled the file "Billy Blood" and tucked it into a desk drawer.

It was warm out, so he took his laptop onto the balcony, leaving the French doors open. Digging around on the Web, he found that Billy Blood had made some bizarre claims about its product, couched in language that wouldn't attract a false advertising lawsuit but that implied nonetheless that the unique proteins in goat's blood provided mental clarity and focus, improved sexual prowess, and even induced weight loss. It was all outrageously, transparently false, but that didn't seem to matter to investors. Dozens of financial news sources had covered the IPO and the shocking amount of money it had attracted.

He turned to detractors and enemies of the company. There wasn't much from Wall Street, apart from one analyst who thought the stock was overvalued out of the gate. But Billy Blood was definitely on the radar of animal rights groups, who discussed it extensively in articles and posts. Nothing he found seemed vociferous enough to foment an attack, and nothing mentioned vandalism.

When he heard Ned come home, he folded his laptop closed and went inside.

"Meetings?" Mason asked him.

"Yeah, I had to go downtown for a few hours. Peggy texted that she won't be home for dinner. Should we go out? I was thinking maybe that vegan soul food place in Inglewood. We can never go there with her. Last time I mentioned it, she said, 'No way—I put on five pounds just driving by that place.'"

"Her loss," Mason said. "Let me change my shirt."

Soon they were heading out in Ned's classic early-seventies Barracuda, which he navigated skillfully down the hill to the freeway. The evening traffic was heavy, as it always was, so they had ample time to chat and catch up. Mason told him about his visit to Billy Blood and getting hired by the CEO.

"You're really OK with working for a company that sells animal products?" Ned said.

"It's not ideal," Mason said, not masking his irritation. "I know it's an abhorrent product. But I have to hustle for the work I get. I can't really turn it down."

"Whoa—I'm not trying to pick a fight," Ned said, glancing over at him.

"Well, you don't seem very supportive."

"You're taking money from a company that's selling goat's blood. I can't pretend to be happy about that."

"I don't think anyone can be completely insulated from animal exploitation, unless you were completely insulated from society. Maybe the point is to change things, not avoid them."

"Will you really be changing anything by working for this guy?" Ned asked.

"Probably not," he said, and turned to look out the window.

"You know, I support your choices, despite what I think about them," Ned said finally.

"That sounds more like tolerance than support," Mason said. He took a deep breath and tried to let it go. "I'm definitely going to get a wad of cash out of this deal. After he told me how much the IPO had raised, I asked for a thousand bucks a day, and he didn't even bother to negotiate. He also didn't make anything contingent on finding answers."

"Obviously they can afford it."

"There's so much money there—can you believe Wall Street valued the company at over a billion dollars and they only have nineteen employees? It means each of those people is worth, like, seventy million dollars."

"Not really. It just means investors think the

company can generate even more money than that, regardless of who's doing the work—people or robots or software."

"Isn't it scary, though, that all those resources are concentrated in so few hands?"

"Sure, but that's the trend in a lot of industries now. Vast amounts of wealth are coagulating in companies that don't create any jobs. Welcome to the new gilded age."

It was a depressing thought. Mason turned back to the window to watch the city crawling by.

"So nobody took credit for defacing the billboards?" Ned said. "Usually when someone goes to all that trouble, they want to get attention for their cause or their organization."

"I know. I thought maybe some animal rights group would claim it indirectly, but none of them seemed particularly riled up about Billy Blood. I found lots of denunciations, but no call to action."

"So maybe it was just plain old vandalism—bored kids or something."

"Maybe," Mason said. "But it seemed too organized. There were incidents at five places on three different nights, spaced a few days apart."

"Well, you have a great track record. I'm sure you'll figure it out."

After they'd filled up on soul food, traffic was fluid on the freeways. Mason settled into the passenger seat and clicked on the radio to find *Metro Grooves,* a nightly program of the house music that he loved. He set the volume low, and they rode home in comfortable silence.

He climbed into bed with Ned and soon found himself drifting into the hypnagogic state, sleep encroaching on his drowsy mind. "Wake up in the dream," he told himself.

Soon he was in the woods, walking along a path bordering a river. It was lush along the bank, but the hills above him were carpeted with dry grass. The imagery was vivid, and he came to awareness in the dream. It didn't destabilize, as it often did when he started to interact consciously with the dream world. He looked around, trying to assess what this place meant. It looked like rural California. A little way along the path he spotted someone crouched over the marshy land at the river's edge. Moving closer, he saw that it was a man, with long hair and grubby, ill-fitting clothes. A homeless person, Mason thought. The man was collecting plants, individual little stalks of something bright green. He looked up at Mason, momentarily startled, and Mason saw he was fairly young and wore the beginnings of a beard.

"Greetings, traveler," the man said. Mason knew he was speaking Spanish, but in the dream state he could understand perfectly.

"You're real," Mason said. "I thought you were a hallucination, but you seem real."

He looked Mason over quickly, then said, "I know you."

"How do you know me? I don't know you."

The man's eyes narrowed. "I don't think you're supposed to be here," he said. "I need more time."

"Dude," Mason said, "I have no agenda with you. I don't really know what's going on," but before he could finish the thought, the scene disintegrated and was gone.

Mason forced himself to wake up to record the details. "Homeless guy," he wrote on the pad from his nightstand. "Real. I'm not supposed to be there. More time."

Tuesday

"Damn it," Mason snapped, dragged into consciousness by his ringing cell phone. It was programmed to stay silent until nine a.m., so he knew it wasn't the middle of the night, even though it felt like it. He grabbed the phone from his nightstand—9:18 a.m.

He cleared his throat, so he wouldn't sound like he'd been awoken, and answered, "Braithwaite."

"Good morning," a bubbly sounding man responded. "My name is Arko Ramsey, and Mr. Frey here at Billy Blood asked me to connect with you today. I'm very excited that we'll be working together."

"OK," Mason said, trying to absorb the information. His tongue felt thick, and his head hurt.

"So if you'd be able to swing by headquarters this morning, we can get started."

"This morning?" Mason said, alarmed at the idea. "Can we aim for a bit later? Around two o'clock?"

"But there's so much to do," Arko protested. "I think we should try to get started ASAP. As soon as possible."

"I know what ASAP stands for," Mason said. "I'll be there as soon as I can."

Morning people, he thought. It always put him in a dark mood when he had to wake up on someone else's timetable. And maybe Peggy was right about soul food; his head throbbed like he'd been drinking. He dragged himself out of bed and popped a couple of ibuprofen before he went out to the kitchen to make coffee. Ned was at work at his desk, and Mason stuck his head in briefly to say hello.

After a couple of pots of coffee and some farmers market blood oranges and strawberries, he started to feel awake enough to leave the house. He pulled on his backpack and kissed Ned good-bye, then went out to the garage to get on his bicycle. The marine layer was still hanging over the city, but with no threat of rain it cast mellow gray light, spreading a little yin energy over the yanged-out metropolis until it burned off after lunch. Even without sunshine, Mason felt invigorated coasting down the hill, and shifted his mind into a positive frame. This was a big new job, after all—how great was that?

Twenty minutes later, he had locked his bicycle

in front of the Billy Blood building and trotted up the front steps. The receptionist remembered him and greeted him with a smile. He asked for Arko, and a few minutes later the man appeared, dressed in a fashionably tight gabardine suit, his hair carefully coiffed. Mason felt underdressed in comparison, in khakis and a short-sleeved shirt, but he knew it didn't really matter.

"Mr. Braithwaite," Arko greeted him.

He was chirpy and upbeat, Mason thought, but not slick like a salesman.

"It's just Mason," he said. "Mr. Braithwaite sounds like my dad."

"Got it," Arko said, and nodded. "Shall we sit for a minute before we head out?" He gestured to the Barcelona chairs near the reception desk.

Mason pulled off his backpack and gingerly sat in one of them, settling his weight gradually. Designers loved these, he knew, but like most things beloved of the fashion-conscious, the chair was completely impractical and uncomfortable, and the last thing he wanted was to flatten the delicate little thing.

"It's so exciting to be working with a psychic," Arko said, beaming, taking the other chair. "Can you tell me something psychic? What am I thinking right now?"

Mason held his index fingers to his temples and closed his eyes for a moment. "I'm sensing that your mind is as clear and unpolluted as a cloudless blue sky on a summer day."

Arko laughed loudly, throwing his head back. "I love it. I'm sure it's hard to be put on the spot like that."

"Arko is an Akan name—is your family Akan?"

"Actually my name is from Ghana."

"Same thing," Mason said. "The Akan live in Ghana."

"Seriously? How do you know that, and I don't even know that?"

"I backpacked around that part of the world when I was fresh out of college. It's a common name there."

"My parents were into the whole Mother Africa thing, but they never went there. Should I go?"

"You'd have to be closeted—it's not safe for gay people."

"How did you know I was gay?" Arko said, genuinely surprised.

"I'm psychic, remember?" Mason said, and smiled, but even Helen Keller would have made that assumption with a cursory glance.

Arko laughed again. "I like you. I wasn't sure if I would. I thought you'd be all, like, crystals and hemp."

"Well, I guess some of us have to break stereotype."

Arko nodded, his brow furrowed thoughtfully. "So—down to business. I know you've seen the case file."

"Frey gave me a copy. Are you his assistant?"

"No—I should have introduced myself properly. I'm in charge of public relations and customer service."

"Both?" Mason asked. With only nineteen employees, maybe they each wore a couple of different hats.

"Mostly I do PR. Customer service isn't very time-consuming."

"I've waded through your phone system, so I know you never have to talk to anyone."

Arko nodded. "We prefer that people visit the website if they need information about the product."

"Or they could just read the side of the can."

"Exactly," he said, and shifted in his chair. "Since you've read through the file, I thought I might drive you to a couple of the sites where we were attacked. You can soak up the vibes, or whatever it is that you do, and maybe interview a shop owner. How does that sound?"

"Great," Mason said. "Let's roll."

"I just have to send a quick text," he said, and thumb-typed on his phone for a moment before leading Mason to the elevator and down to the parking lot under the building. He held up his car keys, and when he pressed the unlock button, a tiny acid-yellow Prius, plastered with the Billy Blood logo, chirped in response.

"Are you going to fit?" Arko asked, looking Mason over dubiously as he opened the driver's side door.

"Sure," Mason said. "My roommate has this exact car." He climbed in and pushed the seat all the way back. "She doesn't keep hers quite as immaculate as you do, though."

"This is a company car," Arko said, and aimed it up the ramp, the tiny engine straining to make it up to street level.

"Who do you think is doing this?" Mason asked him. "The vandalism, I mean."

"I have no idea. It's sad, though, that people get so uptight about a little bit of blood in an energy drink. You can't even taste it. Do you know how much blood is in a steak, or a hot dog? People don't hesitate to eat steaks."

"No, they don't," Mason said.

Arko pulled the car over at a parking meter. They were still on Sunset, not six blocks from the Billy Blood office.

"We're here?" Mason asked, incredulous. They could have walked it in a few minutes.

"Yep," Arko said, and jumped out of the vehicle. "Up there." He pointed back down the boulevard, in the direction they'd come from.

It was hard to miss—the billboard towered over the neighborhood, with the now-familiar lurid logo next to a goat's head, painted over in bright pink: "Leave the goats alone." There were photos of it in the material Frey had given him, but the location was interesting: it couldn't have been more than a block from the Billy Blood office. Entertainment companies often did that, buying advertising space for their own movies and TV shows near the studios where they were produced, as a way to congratulate themselves and boost worker morale. Perhaps Frey's background was in the entertainment industry. Arko fit that mold too, he thought, glancing at him as he stood on the sidewalk, absorbed in his phone. Mason focused on the billboard, trying to be receptive to any insight that might be floating around, but nothing came to mind.

"The file said this happened a while ago," Mason said finally. "Why didn't you have it papered over?"

"So people could see what happened to us. It's a terror attack, and the world needs to know that we've been victimized."

"You sound like your boss," Mason said. Hopefully he was just parroting Frey and didn't really believe that some paint on a billboard qualified as an act of terror.

Mason looked around at the shops and the street, the traffic streaming by. Across the street, in front of the Israeli café, he noticed a camera lens pointed out the window of a black SUV. It had a square lens hood, so it was probably a video camera, and it seemed like it was pointed right at him. That was unnerving. He stared back, but the camera didn't move. There were a lot of those in this town, he decided, and it wasn't illegal to film people standing on the sidewalk gawking at billboards.

"You said something about interviewing a shopkeeper?" he asked Arko.

"Yes. His shop was hit the same night as the billboard. It's not far."

"Is it closer than five blocks?" Mason asked.

"It's right up the street. You can see it from here."

"Then let's walk."

"Really?" he said, his eyes narrowing. "Why?"

"Because you're already parked. Drop a few bucks in the meter, and we'll walk."

Arko complied, shaking his head as if mystified. He walked beside Mason in silence for a minute, and then said, "I remember your shirt."

"Dude, I just met you this morning, remember?"

"I mean, I remember the collection it was in. Sciocche showed it in Milan in their menswear line two seasons back."

"That's distinctly possible. The original owner might have bought it from Sciocche, but I bought it at a thrift store."

"I see," Arko said, sympathy in his eyes, and lapsed into silence.

Mason glanced at him. He had never heard of that designer, but it was impressive that Arko had recognized it. The guy had a good memory for things that were important to him.

"It's interesting that both places you're taking me to are on the same strip as your office," Mason said.

"Not surprising. Sunset is the only street that really matters."

"For Billy Blood? I thought you were going to take it national."

"For everything. If you had to pinpoint the center of the universe, it would be right back there, at Sunset and Laurel Canyon."

"OK," Mason said, unsure if he was joking. A glance at his expression told him that he wasn't. "Can you expand on that?"

"Think of all the creators of culture around here. All the musicians back in the sixties, and since then the filmmakers and TV people. Directors, producers, real housewives. It's all focused on that intersection—it's ground zero."

"Not everyone in this town is in the entertainment business," Mason said.

"If they're not, they're not all that important."

"Do you consider your job part of that industry?" Mason asked. "Is hyping sugar water a form of entertainment?"

"Of course." Arko frowned. "And it's misleading to call it sugar water. It's an aspirational lifestyle drink—it's for people who want to be glamorous."

"I'm not convinced draining goats of their blood is in any way glamorous."

"We're here," Arko said, and pulled open the door for him with a sweet smile, done discussing glamour.

Mason stepped in ahead of him. It was a crowded little liquor store, with snacks and soft drinks on tall shelves in the middle and booze around the outside walls. Arko went to the back and summoned the owner. They had clearly met before.

"This is Mr. Sargasian," Arko said. "This is Mason. He's investigating the damage to the Billy Blood products." The guy was older and looked Mediterranean, but the name sounded Armenian.

Sargasian nodded. "I'll show you."

He returned moments later with a six-pack of Billy Blood in hand, the cans bound together at the top by plastic rings. Stenciled across three of the cans was the same message as the billboard, in the familiar shade of pink, a few sloppy drips running down. Mason had already seen the photos in Frey's file, but he took the six-pack and touched the paint. It had been sprayed on.

"I've got two dozen more of those in the storeroom," Sargasian said.

"You didn't see the vandal," Mason asked, "or get a video of it happening?"

He shook his head. "I missed it. It wasn't busy, and I was working alone. I didn't see it until later— they spray-painted the whole damn display, paint on every can."

"It can't be a big financial loss, though, a few cans of this stuff," Mason said, looking at the six-pack again. "More of an annoyance, right?"

"That stuff retails for six-fifty a can."

"Are you kidding me?" Mason said, shocked.

"No, I'm not. It's several hundred bucks out of my pocket. I can't sell paint-damaged cans, either. That's in the vendor contract."

Mason nodded. "Can I have a minute alone with these? I want to read them."

Sargasian looked confused, but Arko said, "Of course. We'll be up at the register," and put his hand on the shopkeeper's shoulder to steer him away.

It was a long shot, and he'd never done psychometry on an aluminum can before, but it was worth a try. He held the six-pack close to his eyes so that he could read the tiny print on the side of one of the tall, slender cans. The ingredient list was lengthy, mostly indecipherable chemical names, and the nutrition listed was a lot of zeros, apart from sodium and a startling carbohydrate count—the stuff must be loaded with sugar.

He closed his eyes and took a couple of deep breaths, holding both ends of the six-pack in his hands. He cleared his mind, gradually brushing away the random noise, and waited for insight to trickle in. It took a while, pushing down spurious thoughts, but eventually an image formed—the head of a goat, like the one painted over on the billboard, with floppy ears and those weird irises. It bleated loudly.

He opened his eyes. That wasn't especially helpful, although it was clearly related. Then he noticed, at the end of the aisle, half obscured behind a rack of potato chips, a guy with a video camera, the square lens hood pointed directly at Mason.

"What are you doing?" Mason called to him.

"Just ignore me," the cameraman said, looking up from his lens. "Act natural."

"What the hell? Stop filming me," he said, but the camera didn't budge. "Are you the one who was filming us from across the street?"

The cameraman didn't respond but gestured for Mason to go back to what he'd been doing.

"Mr. Sargasian," he called toward the register, "did you know there was a film crew in your store?"

Arko appeared at the end of the aisle, followed by Sargasian, who didn't speak but looked thoroughly cowed. For whatever reason, he was going along with it.

"He's with Billy Blood," Arko said cheerfully. "Didn't I mention that? We record all our research work."

"You didn't," Mason said. He looked back to the camera. It was still trained on him, unwavering. "Dude, I didn't agree to this." But he knew that he had—it had to have been in the nondisclosure agreement he'd signed.

"I should have said something—my bad. But let's not get upset," Arko said.

"Let's not spring things on me surreptitiously," Mason said. Before Arko could reply, he added, "I've learned all I can here anyway, so it's time to go."

"You can keep the six-pack," Sargasian said.

Mason looked down at his hands. He'd forgotten he was still holding it.

The camera swung around toward Sargasian. "Could you say that again?" the cameraman asked.

"You can keep the six-pack," he said again, exactly as he had the first time, looking at Mason rather than the camera. He'd obviously done this before.

"On me," Arko said, and after the camera was trained on him, with a concerned look he said, "Have you got what you need?"

"I just said I did," Mason said, frowning.

"I know—it's to edit in later," Arko said. "We'll run my question before your answer. It'll make the record more robust."

This was getting surreal, and Mason had no intention of working in front of a camera. He brushed past the cameraman, handing the cans to Sargasian as he headed out the door.

"Let me get set up outside, so I can film you walking out," the cameraman called after Mason.

"Hold on," Arko said, following Mason out to the street and catching up with him. "I wasn't trying to trick you. I just forgot to explain it. It's not a big deal."

"OK," Mason said, not breaking his stride. He wasn't sure if he believed the guy, but he sounded sincere. Still, he wasn't ready to be on reality TV. "From now on, though, I'm going to work independently. Unless there's something more I need to see?"

"No, but let me drive you back to the office. The boss wanted us to cut you a check."

They climbed into Arko's little car and made their way back to the Billy Blood office. Mason could have walked it more quickly than it took to get turned around on the side streets and headed back the other direction on the boulevard.

They drove in silence, and Arko seemed a little stressed out, massaging the steering wheel with both hands. Finally he said, "So I'm going to this thing tonight, and I wondered if you wanted to come with."

"Is it a Billy Blood thing? Will you be filming me?"

"It's not for work—it's this wet tighty-whitey contest, at a bar in Boystown. They have two-for-one tequila shots every Tuesday."

"Are you asking me on a date?" Mason said, incredulous.

"In a way," Arko said, looking flustered now. "Unless you're not into it, then no, I'm not."

"You are asking me out," Mason said, and laughed. "I'm totally flattered."

"So is that a yes?" Arko asked, looking over at Mason.

"That contest sounds thoroughly inspired—but I'm partnered, and we're exclusive, so I can't. But thank you for asking me."

"I didn't know you had a boyfriend," he said. "Forget I asked."

"I'm not going to forget. That never happens to me, and I love it."

Arko pulled the car into the garage at the Billy Blood building and they climbed out. "So I don't have to be embarrassed?" he asked.

"No way. Dude, you made my day."

They rode up to the lobby together, Mason still smiling to himself.

As they arrived, Arko said, "If you don't mind waiting here, I'll go up and get your check. It should be ready."

Mason stepped off the elevator and wandered over to the front desk. He greeted the receptionist, who stood when she saw him.

"Don't get up," he said. "I'm just waiting for Arko. He'll be right down."

"Have a seat, if you'd like," she said, and then added, "It really works."

"What does?" he asked.

"The look you're working. The red hair, and the shirt, and the backpack—it works."

"Thanks," he said, "but I didn't have a lot of choice about the hair. And the shirt is two years old, apparently."

Her eyes narrowed. "I thought that was just part of your look, like, 'I've got other stuff going on, so I don't have time to care that this is an old shirt.'"

"You nailed it," he said, and nodded. "That's exactly the look I'm working."

She smiled, and went back to her desk. How amazing, he thought wryly, that he was working a look and didn't even know it. More impressive was that not being worried about his shirt was so easily mistaken for the affectation of not being worried about his shirt. On top of that, he had been paid two compliments in rapid succession today, if appreciation of his hair color counted as a compliment. It did, he decided. He wandered to the front windows and watched the cars passing on the boulevard. Maybe that was too much of a coincidence, though—two of Frey's employees massaging his ego today. He thought about it. Maybe he was being paranoid, and should just accept it at face value. Frey had nothing to gain by yanking Mason's chain.

Arko arrived, and handed him an envelope. "My understanding is that the balance is payable on delivery of your report," he said.

"That's the deal I made with Frey," Mason said, stuffing the envelope into his backpack. "Have fun tonight on your outing."

"I'm not sure I'll go alone," Arko said, looking sheepish.

"You should. It sounds like a great place to meet single guys. And weeknights are the best time to go out."

"Why is that?"

"Saturday is amateur night—everyone goes out. But people who go out on weeknights are serious about having fun."

"Hmm. I'll have to think about that," he said, but he smiled amicably when Mason said good-bye.

He had just unlocked his bike when a voice behind him said, "Mason B. Fancy seeing you here." He knew that voice. He turned to look, and sure enough, it was Laura, a fellow traveler in the psychic world that he'd met out in the desert a few weeks earlier. She had advanced paranormal skills that he had only a vague understanding of: she was a bona fide time traveler. He wasn't sure how she managed it, but with her help he'd been able to allow his consciousness to bleed through to the past, to gather firsthand information for a case he was working. Today she was dressed for camping, just the way he'd seen her last, in jeans and a plaid shirt, and her dark hair looked as dry and brittle as it had in the desert.

"You're the last person I expected to see today," he said. "What are you doing here?"

"Looking for you, chum. Where are you headed?"

"I'm going downtown, but I was going to get lunch first."

"Great, I'm starving," she said, and moments later they were walking toward a Thai place up the street, Mason wheeling his bicycle along between them.

"It's good to see you," he said. She seemed focused and present, which hadn't always been the case. "So why were you looking for me?"

"I wanted to debrief about what happened out in the desert, if you'll indulge me."

"We already did that."

"Of course," she said, "but perhaps you could remind me of some of the details."

Mason thought for a minute. "I think I know what's happening. You haven't yet resolved things back then, and you've fast-forwarded here to get the resolution. Next you'll go back then and act it out. You're completely out of sequence."

"That's approximately correct," she said, and grinned. "Did I tell you how I do my work?"

"You did. Or you will, in your timeline. It must be nice to be able to jump ahead like this and get the answers."

"It can be," she said, "but there are costs. Like when you drive your car really fast, you get there sooner, but you burn up way more gas. It causes physiological effects."

They had arrived at the Thai place, and Laura went in to get a table while Mason locked up his bike. He found her seated in the dimly lit interior, near the bar. He settled in and ordered a veggie curry and black coffee; Laura asked for noodles. It felt good to be somewhere darker and more private, no chance of cameras peering at him.

"So what do you want me to tell you?" he asked her.

Laura questioned him about what had happened in the desert, and he narrated his experiences. She interrupted him occasionally to skip over the parts she already knew.

"I think that's all I need," she said finally, setting down her fork and pushing her plate away.

"Doesn't it get confusing to live your life out of sequence?" he asked her.

"You get used to it. I guess the hard part is connecting with people—maintaining friendships. I wanted to talk to you about that too. You should connect with other people in our field."

"I guess I never really thought about having peers. It feels like my psychic stuff is personal, not really a social thing."

"I'm not saying you should join the Rotary Club. But there are lots of people active in the field, and you could learn a lot."

"Like what?" Mason asked, gesturing to the

waiter for a refill on his coffee.

"Have you heard of something called direction-finding?" she asked.

"I don't think so."

"It's a psychic way to locate something that's lost or misplaced. You focus on a mental image of the item, then open your mind, without filtering what's flowing through it. Around the edges of your awareness you'll notice information that will tell you which direction to go, and where to look."

"That does sound useful," Mason said. It was intriguing—he'd never even heard of it, but the technique sounded similar to some of the other ways he obtained insight.

"You probably wouldn't have found it easily on your own, but now you have a new tool at your disposal, just from hanging out with me for a little while."

"From the way you describe it, I know it'll work," he said.

"There's more to learn. Doing your own thing feels comfortable, but sometimes you have to push beyond that."

"You sound like my shrink," he said.

She laughed. "I'm glad you're hearing it from more than one source. It's good advice: be social. You should go see Hanh. Her shop is right up the street."

Hanh was Ned's manicurist, but she was also a psychic practitioner. Inexplicably, she'd found Mason when he was adrift in his first psychic bleed-through, and pressed him to complete his task. She hadn't been very friendly, though, and she certainly wasn't the first person Mason wanted to socialize with.

"She can come and see me, if she wants to," he said.

Laura sighed. "It's more than just a suggestion, Mason. I'm asking you to go see her specifically because she needs your help, even though she doesn't know it yet."

He believed her, without reservation. From the time they'd spent together, he trusted her abilities. He knew she wouldn't ask if it wasn't important. "Is it urgent?" he asked.

"Well, let's say within the next forty-eight hours or so, you two should have a chat."

He nodded. "I'll stop by her place tomorrow," he said. "Can I ask what it's about?"

"Ask her," she said. "I only know the broad strokes."

The waiter set the bill on the table, and Laura folded her napkin and dropped it on her plate.

"Can you get this?" she asked, rising to leave. "I don't have any money."

"Sure," Mason said, and pulled his wad of cash out of his pants pocket, peeling off the appropriate bills. He followed her out to the street.

"I'm glad we got caught up," she said.

"So why today, and why here?" he asked. "Why not come and see me last week, or next week? You're not limited by time the way most of us are—you could have looked me up whenever."

"Well, the thing with Hanh came up," she said. "Plus, I knew where you'd be."

"How did you know that?"

"That's about the future, so it's off-limits." She smiled.

He knew it was pointless to question her further; he'd just have to accept that she couldn't explain everything. He doubted he'd even understand it if she tried.

"Will I see you again?" he asked.

"Of course." She flashed a smile and turned away, walking back up Sunset.

Mason watched her for a few moments and then unlocked his bike. When he'd started on this journey he probably should have expected that strange things would start happening, and odd people would show up in his life, but he was still getting used to it. So much of the work, his psychic experiences, seemed to be subconscious, which made it feel like he had no control over them. That didn't mean he wasn't getting better at it—he knew that he was. But the deeper he dove, the weirder things got.

He cycled to the metro and locked up his bike at the station, then rode the train downtown to the central library. He planned to do some more research on animal rights groups and determine whether any of them had a vendetta against Billy Blood. He'd only heard of a handful of them, and as he got into it, sitting in the history department reading news clippings, he found there were far more of them than he'd imagined. They ran the gamut from mainstream to radical, international to neighborhood-based, but he couldn't find anything about anyone targeting Billy Blood. In a way, it made sense, since the company had just gone public and hadn't yet become a major player in the sugary drink market.

A couple of hours of reading about animal rights activism brought him to the conclusion that none of these groups would pull a stunt like defacing a billboard without taking credit. Whenever they acted publicly, they wanted the ensuing attention, to highlight their name and their spin on the issues. The pink paint job might have been done by an individual, maybe a street artist. But that didn't make sense either: street artists used stylized lettering and signed their work with idiosyncratic tags. The pink paint on the Billy Blood billboard didn't look like that. Something else was going on, and it had nothing to do with street artists, or animal rights groups, and certainly not terrorists.

When he got home, Peggy and Ned were collaborating on dumplings stuffed with spinach and a lemony soy dipping sauce. He helped them carry everything to the dining table and then sat with them to enjoy the meal. The sun had gone down, but it was a warm evening, so Ned pulled open the French doors to let in the air.

Mason told them about meeting Arko, and visiting the liquor store, and the unsettling feeling of being filmed.

"What are they going to do with the footage?" Peggy asked.

"I have no idea. Maybe it's just for their records, or maybe to show the boss what my techniques are."

"The Arko guy didn't explain why they were recording?" she said.

"I didn't ask. I was kind of flustered at seeing the camera, so I bolted. And then when we went back to the office," Mason said, grinning at the memory, "he asked me out."

"On a date?" Ned said, incredulous.

"Yes. He invited me to a wet tighty-whitey contest at a bar in Boystown."

"Are you going?" Ned asked, deftly grabbing another dumpling with his chopsticks.

"Of course not. I told him I had the sober version of all that waiting at home."

"You seem happy about it," Peggy said.

"You're a woman, so guys hit on you all the time, at the gas station or wherever. But it never happens to me. So, score."

"That's not a good thing, by the way, getting hit on at the gas station," she said.

"I'm sure it would get annoying. But it's so unusual for me, it's a little ego boost."

"And why do they need to have a wet tighty-whitey contest?" she asked, passing Mason the plate of dumplings. "It's so much easier these days for gay guys just to be out without focusing on sex. Why not have a trivia night or something? The underwear thing seems so tacky."

"That's part of what the struggle was for," Ned said. "So guys like Arko could have wet underwear contests without fear of getting arrested or getting their heads bashed in. There's room for sex along with everything else."

"Would you go to an event like that?" Peggy asked.

"Maybe," Ned said. "It seems kind of ditzy. But it's good that people can be open and do whatever they want."

Mason helped clean up, then went into the office and turned on his laptop. He wanted to make another attempt to find Catherine. She was probably getting worried about her stuff by now. He looked at the photo he'd taken of her rental contract, and looked online for the rental company's phone number. He dialed and spoke to a sales agent, and got transferred to an insurance office, and spent some time wading through a voice mail labyrinth. Finally he got connected to an adjuster.

Once Mason had explained the situation, the adjuster said, "Even if I could look in that file, I couldn't give you her contact info. What if you're some crazy person stalking this woman?"

"What's crazy is that I have her briefcase and can't get it back to her," Mason said. "Any suggestions?"

"Drop it off at the agency where she rented the car."

It wasn't a bad idea. He pulled up the photo of her rental contract, and found that it had a code for the office where she'd picked up the car: "SBT." A Web search revealed that to be the airport in San Bernardino, hours of freeway driving to the east. He definitely wasn't going to schlep out there, but maybe Catherine had spoken to someone in that office about her missing stuff. He found the number for the place and dialed, and a recording told him it was past their business hours, then hung up on him.

Ned poked his head in and said, "You look busy."

"Have you ever heard of the San Bernardino airport?"

"Sure. It's a white elephant: they built a terminal and gates and all the infrastructure, but there are no passenger flights in or out. It's an empty building."

"Seriously? That woman who rear-ended me on the freeway rented her car there."

"Well, she didn't come in on a commercial flight. Freight companies use it, and the military, but none of the airlines."

That seemed strange, but it didn't really help him find her. He would call the rental office again in the morning, he decided, and put the matter aside.

When he got into bed later, Ned playfully climbed up and straddled him. "So who's hotter, gumshoe? Me or the tighty-whitey guy?"

"No comparison," Mason said. "Ned wins by a mile."

"Good answer," he said, and Mason pulled him down for a kiss.

Mason wondered if Ned initiating sex was a reaction to someone else taking an interest in him, a way of making sure he wouldn't be tempted to stray. That wasn't even a consideration for Mason, but whatever the reason, the intimacy was welcome.

Drifting into sleep, he tried to induce a dream about the billboard vandalism and the stenciled drink cans, focusing on the spray-painted words in his mind. Later, he came to awareness and realized he was in the office of Miss Cassie, his shrink. It was all below him, her desk and her furniture. He must be floating up near the ceiling. She had been his first client as a psychic investigator, and later she had cajoled him into becoming her client, so they had something more than a professional relationship; he had seen inside her personal life. It was dark outside her windows, and disturbingly, Ned was there, sitting on her sofa, engaged in earnest conversation with her. Unlike in Mason's sessions with Miss Cassie, she was doing a lot of the talking, but he couldn't hear either one of them. They didn't know he was there, floating above them, and it was frustrating not to know what was being said. He decided he didn't want to try to engage with them—it felt too private.

Eventually the image destabilized, and Mason willed himself awake to record the details. "Ned and Miss Cassie," he wrote on his bedside notepad, "intent conversation." Ned had never met her, as far as Mason knew, but was it possible that they had? No, he decided, his groggy mind sinking back toward sleep. A more likely explanation was that his subconscious mind feared that there was something in Ned that he couldn't trust. Even though it almost certainly wasn't real, the idea of the two of them conspiring made him uneasy.

Wednesday

"You should get up," Ned said. Mason started awake to find Ned sitting next to him on the bed, dressed for a day out at meetings, holding a coffee mug. Mason sat up, and Ned pressed the mug into his hands.

"What's going on?" he asked, annoyed—despite the presence of coffee—to be awoken so early in the day.

"Don't freak out," Ned said, "but there's something you should see."

"When you tell me not to freak out, it makes me feel freaked out. What is it?"

"It might be good news, and it might be bad news. I'll be in the kitchen when you're ready," Ned said, and walked out.

Mason gulped some of the coffee, trying to shake off his irritation at Ned's mysterious summons, and got up, stumbling into his clothes. He went into the front room, and found Ned had his tablet set up on the counter.

"I queued the video," Ned called from the kitchen. "It was on the local news about half an hour ago. Just press 'play.' I'll make you some oatmeal."

It must be serious, Mason thought, if he was getting breakfast out of the deal. He sat on a bar stool and started the video. It was a local news segment that began with the coiffed reporter standing on the sidewalk, the familiar defaced Billy Blood billboard visible in the distance over her shoulder.

"Poised to flood the market with an exciting new lifestyle product," she began, "here in Los Angeles, Billy Blood has found itself on the receiving end"— she paused for dramatic effect—"of some harsh criticism." The camera zoomed in on the billboard, the pink words of protest over the image of the goat, next to the acid-yellow product logo.

"I was right there yesterday," Mason said. "Why would this freak me out?"

Ned looked up from the stove. "Keep watching," he said.

The video cut to Frey, standing in the lobby of the Billy Blood building, the product logo above the reception desk neatly positioned behind him in the video frame. The caption at the bottom of the screen said "Tyler Frey, Billy Blood CEO."

"Do you have any insight into who mounted this attack?" the reporter asked, deep concern in her eyes.

The image cut back to Frey. "Not yet, but we know it was a coordinated hit. Terrorism takes many forms, and an attack on Billy Blood is an attack on civilization itself. But I assure you: we will not be intimidated."

"I understand you've taken an unconventional path in your investigation," she said.

"We have a responsibility to our consumers to do everything in our power to find out who's behind this. We will leave no stone unturned," he said.

The video cut to a grainy close-up of a six-pack of Billy Blood, stenciled over in pink paint, then pulled out to reveal who was holding it. Red hair, a very familiar shirt—it took a moment to register that Mason was looking at himself.

"No," he said softly.

"In an effort to identify the vandals, Billy Blood has hired a local psychic," the reporter said in the voiceover. For what seemed like an eternity, the video showed Mason standing there, holding the six-pack, eyes screwed shut, a pained expression on his face. The caption at the bottom identified him as "Nelson Wrathway, psychic consultant."

Mason paused the video, freezing the image of him in front of racks of soft drinks and snacks, and stared at it. "I look like someone just dropped a hammer on my foot. Do I always look like that?" he demanded.

"Well, you're doing your psychic thing," Ned said, "so you just look like you're concentrating."

"I look like an idiot," Mason snapped. Almost as bad as having his face broadcast all over town was his slept-on hair, his ill-fitting trousers—until this moment he had no notion of what other people saw.

"At least now you know why the camera was there," Ned said, setting a bowl of oatmeal in front of Mason and handing him a spoon.

"I'm such an idiot. They had me sign something that gave them rights to use images of me. At the time I didn't even realize what that meant."

"I love how they misspelled your name."

"It's totally insulting. They make me look stupid, and mangle my name while they're at it."

"Actually, that's the best part—no one who sees this will be able to track you down."

Mason considered that. "I guess that is a good thing," he admitted. He stared at himself on the screen, frozen in awkward concentration.

"You should watch the rest," Ned said. "And eat. I'll make another pot of espresso."

He pressed "play," fearful that it might get worse. The video cut to a clip of him standing on the sidewalk in front of Arko's company clown car, out-of-focus vehicles dramatically whizzing by in the foreground. Mason was in profile, his hands on his hips, staring into the distance. Arko was in the frame as well, looking the same direction Mason was, his suit falling perfectly over his frame, as if he'd just stepped out of a fashion shoot; Mason looked more like he'd just been rescued after several days lost in the wilderness. He paused the playback and took it all in.

"Do I always slouch like that?" he asked Ned.

"You didn't know the camera was on you, so you're not at your best," he said.

"That's not an answer," he said. "And why do my pants fit like that?"

"We can go shopping, if you need pants," Ned said.

Mercifully the video quickly cut back to the reporter, asking, "Have you seen any results from your psychic consultant?"

"We're certain that our research will pan out," Frey said, smiling confidently at her, "but I'm not at liberty to discuss the specifics of our investigation at this time."

Mason half listened to the reporter winding up the story, making sure there was no more footage of him. He folded the tablet closed and dug into the oatmeal, and Ned refilled his coffee mug. He knew it was pure vanity, but it was shocking that his self-image was so far from what he saw in that video. But that's what nature had set him up with, and he would have to work on integrating the uncomfortable truth.

"What am I going to do?" he said finally.

"Do you think they intentionally misled you?" Ned asked.

He thought for a minute. "No. I think they

probably just film everything, hoping to get some media attention, and this was the story that did it. Arko knew the camera guy was there, but he completely ignored him, like he was always around." He sighed. "It's my own fault for not questioning what I signed, and not asking what the camera was for."

"So there's your answer," Ned said. "There's not much you can do. It's upsetting, and you can tell them that, but it's already been broadcast. It'll probably run a few more times today, unless there's a good car chase or something, and that'll be the end of it. At least they got your name wrong."

Mason finished his oatmeal and went into the office, plunking down behind his desk. It was mortifying to see unflattering images of himself on television, but he knew Ned was right: he had no grounds to feel betrayed, when what was happening should have been obvious. But he was still upset.

He opened his bottom drawer pulled out the file he'd labeled "Billy Blood." He'd thrown Frey's business card inside, and he pulled his phone out of his pants and dialed the number.

Frey had said it was a direct line, but Arko's familiar upbeat voice answered with, "Billy Blood—the all-natural lifestyle drink."

"So I'm watching television this morning," Mason began, "and lo and behold, there's me, on the local news."

"You saw it," Arko said, his tone rising an octave. "I'm glad."

"I'm not glad. How could you expose me like that without asking?"

"I don't understand," Arko said. "It's free publicity for your business. What's the problem?"

"I don't want that kind of publicity."

"But … why not? You're on TV, Billy Blood is on TV. Everybody wins."

"Arko, my anonymity is like a precious china cup. Once it's shattered, it can never be restored."

The line was silent. Finally Arko said, "I understand that you're upset. I'm not sure I understand the whole situation, but I'm hearing your concerns."

It was classic customer-service speak, Mason realized. He wondered if Arko had pulled out a customer-service response template.

"What can we do to make things right today?" Arko asked.

"Stop distributing that video."

"I can't do that," he said flatly, going off-script. "It's like your china cup. It's already out there."

"I figured as much." He sighed. "Next time, just tell people what you're trying to do. Not everybody wants to be on TV."

"Thank you for that feedback. We'll be sure to take that into consideration," he said, reading from the template again. And then, his tone brightening, "So how is your research proceeding?"

"It's going fine. I'm pursuing several leads." It wasn't really true, but if Arko could read from a script, he could too.

"Were you planning to attend the CEO's speech today?" Arko asked.

"He mentioned it on Monday, but I wasn't sure when it was scheduled."

"Your attendance would be appreciated," Arko said. "It starts at eleven."

He didn't really want to listen to Frey championing his foul product, but he still wanted to get paid, and accepting the invitation might give him a chance to get another lead.

"It's at your office?"

"Mimosas in the lobby at ten thirty," Arko said.

"All right—I'll see you then."

He ended the call and stared absently at the photos from the file spread across the surface of his desk. It might not be a waste of time to go over there. Maybe listening to Frey speak would give him some insight. He really did have to dredge up some leads if he was going to figure this out.

He picked up the photo of the six-pack. A pair of hands with stubby fingers and hairy knuckles held it up for the camera. That must be Sargasian. Yesterday the guy had cooperated completely with the cameraman, and he had acted deferentially to Arko. Mason would have interviewed him, but didn't because the camera had appeared. It might be worthwhile to drop by there again and actually talk with the guy this time, and maybe find out how involved he was with the Billy Blood company.

A shower made him feel a lot better, but he was

uneasy about riding around the city after his unexpected TV appearance. He dug around in his dresser drawer before he left and found an old pair of sunglasses with green mirrored lenses. Ned had once said they made him look like an oversize dragonfly, but they helped him feel a bit more incognito.

Having no interest in quaffing mimosas with Frey's employees, he arrived at the Billy Blood office just before eleven. There were a lot of people around the front entrance as he locked up his bicycle. He stepped through the front door and pulled off his sunglasses. There were even more people inside, and most were dressed up beyond normal office attire. The mimosas had obviously taken effect among the crowd, with loud conversations and ringing boisterous laughter giving the lobby the atmosphere of a hotel bar.

Mason scanned the crowd, feeling awkward and out of place. He didn't know anyone, and he was painfully underdressed. A bar was set up at one side of the lobby. He made his way toward it. There were champagne bottles galore, but no orange juice on the bar, only cans of Billy Blood, even an eight-foot tower of six-packs displayed at one end. He glanced around and saw that people were drinking from champagne flutes, but the contents looked uniformly pink; clearly Billy Blood was the only mixer on offer. It was a big stretch to call that a mimosa.

A woman he'd never seen before caught his eye and said, "How are you? Good to see you."

Mason said, "Hello," and smiled at her, but kept walking. He realized she'd probably recognized him from the media coverage. A lot of these people probably knew exactly who he was. He could feel his cheeks burning.

"Mason," a familiar voice called to him, and Arko stepped through the crowd, champagne flute in hand. What a relief.

"This is quite a turnout," Mason said.

"I know, right? People love the product," Arko said, putting his hand in the small of Mason's back. "We're moving into the theater now, so let me find you a seat."

It felt flirty, the physical contact. He grinned and glanced at Arko as they walked. Flattering as it was, more likely Arko was simply in PR mode. Even so, the connection was gratifying. Mason followed him past the elevators toward the back of the building, through a set of double doors into an actual theater. There were maybe two hundred seats, and an elevated stage with black curtains. It seemed like an odd thing to have in an office building, but then again, this was Hollywood. Lots of companies in the industry would put a screening room to good use.

The seats were more than half occupied, and the lobby crowd was filing in to fill the rest. Arko led him to the third row, where several seats had sheets of paper taped to them with the word RESERVED printed in big letters. He deftly ripped the sign off the first seat.

"Why don't you sit on the aisle," he said, "so you have room to stretch your legs. I'll be back in two minutes."

Mason sat, dropping his backpack on the floor at his feet, and turned to look back at the crowd filling the theater. As they had such a small staff, most of these people weren't Billy Blood employees. Some had to be journalists, he reasoned, as there were three different video cameras set up at the back of the hall between the doors, but there were still far more bodies than could be accounted for by staff and media.

He saw the lawyer that he'd met on Monday, Weston, on the other side of the room. She didn't look any less stressed out than she had in her office. A few rows back, a guy caught Mason's eye and mouthed "Hello," as if they were old friends. Mason had never seen him before. He nodded in acknowledgment and turned away, looking up at the empty stage. He called himself a psychic, and even advertised his services, but it was altogether uncomfortable having perfect strangers know who he was, based on a video clip that made him feel foolish.

Arko soon returned, pulled the RESERVED sign off the seat beside him, and settled in. Mason slouched down as much as he could, although with his height and the red hair, it was impossible to be inconspicuous.

"Are you ready?" Arko asked him enthusiastically, a broad smile on his face. He'd clearly been enjoying the "mimosas."

"I can't wait," Mason said. The sentiment was sincere; the sooner focus shifted to the stage, the sooner Mason would feel less on display.

A young woman with fuchsia hair appeared at one side of the stage, standing behind a little table set up there. She pulled on a pair of headphones and in moments the room was filled with the thumping bass of upbeat music. She danced and fiddled with her controls, pointedly ignoring the crowd.

"You hired a DJ?" Mason asked Arko.

"Isn't she amazing?"

The music dropped in volume when the first Billy Blood employee he'd met, Mr. Davis, strode onto the stage, in another immaculate suit, microphone in hand.

"Welcome, Kids and Kid fans," he said, and the audience clapped and whooped.

Arko leaned closer to Mason and explained quietly, "'Kids' is what we call Billy Blood employees."

"All nineteen of them?" Mason asked, but Arko had turned his attention back to Davis.

"Who do we want to see?" Davis said, his voice booming over the music on the sound system.

"Frey!" the crowd shouted.

"Let's give it up for Kid number one, Tyler Frey."

Half the audience were on their feet as Frey strode onstage, waving to them and beaming like a politician. He wore a sharp blue suit with a high-end sheen.

Davis retreated offstage, and Frey waited for

the music and cheering to fade, looking around the crowd, clearly enjoying himself. "There's a lot of love in this room," he said finally. "And I can honestly say that I love each and every one of you with all my heart. You've made Billy Blood what it is today."

It took a minute for the screaming and clapping to subside before he could continue. He didn't speak for long, probably aware that as the alcohol wore off, the enthusiasm of his audience might start to fade. He talked about the product, and how successful the IPO had been, and the coming great expansion. None of it was new to Mason, but it was fascinating to watch the guy work the crowd. He was a good speaker, his delivery polished and present, and he moved around the stage casually, making a point of looking each person in the eye at least once. His audience treated him like a rock star.

He talked about the vandalism—to Mason's disbelief actually using the phrase "haters gonna hate"—and referred to Mason obliquely when he reassured the crowd that the company was using "alternative approaches" to get to the bottom of it. Mason slouched lower in his seat.

Frey wound up with a call to action: "Let's make Billy Blood the hottest lifestyle product in the world," and held his fists high in the air, a tangible vision of victory.

Along with everyone in the room, Arko jumped to his feet, clapping wildly, adoration in his eyes. Mason hesitated but eventually stood up, clapping along with everyone else.

"I love that guy," Arko said, as Frey walked off the stage.

"I can see that," Mason said, and stepped into the aisle.

"We're going to have a buffet lunch in the lobby," he said, as they followed the crowd toward the exits.

"I can't stay, but thanks for inviting me," Mason said.

"That's too bad—there are some people I'd like you to meet. Can you spare five minutes to chat?"

Mason was certain he meant chatting with journalists. "Sorry, I can't," he said. "But I'll be in touch."

Once he was out of the theater he made a beeline through the lobby toward the front door. The table where the bar had been was now piled with platters of food, and a team of uniformed servers stood at the ready. Was that a roasted pig? It was, posed as the lurid centerpiece of the lunch spread. He tried to push the stomach-churning image away as he strode through the building's front doors to freedom.

Once he was outside he was alone again. Everyone else must have been planning to stay for lunch. He put on his sunglasses and unlocked his bike, heading east on Sunset.

Mason didn't know anything about how the beverage industry operated, but that event was an entertainment industry hype fest, with Frey playing the part of the celebrity. Maybe the sugary drink market operated like fast food—there was no qualitative difference among vendors, so the only tool they had to distinguish themselves was marketing and hype.

A few minutes later he found a bike rack on the street a block or so from Sargasian's shop, far enough away to approach the liquor store without putting his mode of transportation on display. He locked up his bike and walked over, pulling off his sunglasses as he stepped into the dim interior. A bewhiskered young man was perched behind the register, engrossed in his phone, but the shop was otherwise deserted.

"Is Sargasian here?" Mason asked.

"In the back," the young man said, glancing up and nodding vaguely.

Mason walked back and rapped on the door marked "Private." A moment later Sargasian pulled it open. He peered up at Mason for a moment, then with a scowl of recognition said, "You're the psychic."

"That's me. My name is Mason."

"I remember. Are you with the camera guy?" he asked, looking warily out into the shop.

"No, I'm on my own. I wanted to ask you about the camera, though."

Sargasian sighed. "Come in," he said, and Mason followed him into the cramped office, where Sargasian gestured to a chair parked at a cluttered table. Mason sat down, setting his backpack on the floor at his feet, and eyed a haphazard stack of Billy Blood six-packs in the corner, all defaced with pink paint.

"I'm going to try to sell those online," Sargasian

explained, "once the perp has been caught and there's more media coverage." He took the other chair and faced Mason, palms on his knees. "So what can I do for Billy Blood Corp today?"

"I'm not here for them. I'm more of an independent investigator," Mason said.

Sargasian frowned. "But you work for Billy Blood."

"Yes, but I'm not representing them. I'm curious about how you're connected to the company, though. Yesterday you seemed comfortable with the camera, like it had been in here before."

"Several times since the attacks," he said.

"It felt like a reality TV show," Mason said. "They were doing multiple takes of the same thing, and trying to set up shots in advance."

"That's how they're filming it, but it's not for a TV show. They document everything for their records and for news coverage." He shrugged. "It's just the way it has to be done."

"You don't seem happy about it. Why not kick them out? It's your shop."

Sargasian's eyes grew wide. "I can't do that. People want this stuff, so I have to carry it. Billy Blood is part of a package deal with my distributor—if I don't carry it, there are thirty other products I can't carry either. So I have to cooperate with the manufacturer. And if they're right about the vandalism, we'll all get some increased sales out of the deal."

Mason nodded. It fit with what he'd seen so far. "You said you were working alone the night the display was vandalized. Do you have any memory of someone coming into the store?"

"I've been through this with the Arko kid."

"I'd like to hear it again, firsthand."

Sargasian sighed. "I know people came in, but I barely registered them, because it wasn't significant in that moment. It was late, and it wasn't busy. The Billy Blood display was in the middle aisle, with the snacks, so not in direct view of the register or the back room. I must have been settling the cash drawer, or something like that, when they hit the display. I honestly can't remember."

Mason nodded. "But you were here, and maybe some part of your mind remembers something more. Would you be willing to be hypnotized? I might be able to draw out some memories."

Sargasian's eyes narrowed. "I saw that done in Vegas," he said. "The hypnotist made a guy's belt turn into a snake."

"I'm not going to do *that*. I'll just put you into a light trance to see if you have any hidden memories of that night."

He watched Mason for a moment, considering. "You won't ask me anything embarrassing?"

"Of course not. Hypnosis is just an altered state of mind to help you focus. I can't make you do or say anything that you don't want to. It's not like you're unconscious—you're still in charge of what's happening."

"That's what the magician in Vegas said too,"

Sargasian said. "Do you know what you're doing? You won't leave me under?"

"Of course not. I'm well versed in the technique." In truth he'd never done it before, but he'd read a couple of books about it when he was researching the tools of his profession. This would be his first attempt to put someone under, but Sargasian didn't need to know that.

"What the hell," the shopkeeper said finally. "Go ahead—knock me out."

"Cool," Mason said. "So, when you want to go somewhere to relax, do you prefer the beach, the desert, or the mountains?"

"I love the desert," he said hesitantly, clearly wondering why Mason was asking.

"OK. First, get comfortable in your chair." He waited while the man settled back. "Next, close your eyes. Feel your whole body relaxing, so that you're completely comfortable." He paused again. "Focus on the sound of my voice. Imagine you're taking a walk in the desert. The weather is perfect, and the sky is clear blue." He spoke for a few minutes about walking in the desert landscape, describing the sand underfoot, the manzanitas and the yuccas, keeping his voice melodic and even. Finally he said, "When you open your eyes, you'll feel even more relaxed. Go ahead, open them."

Sargasian did so, slowly, his expression completely calm. He stared drowsily past Mason's shoulder. It had worked, Mason thought, startled. Focusing on the rhythm of Mason's calm words had brought his mind to a state of trance. He hadn't completely expected that, and he probably should have put more thought into what came next—he had to get the guy to sift through his memories without fabricating or imagining things.

"Think back to the night you found the cans vandalized," he said, choosing his words carefully. "You were in the store all evening. What happened that evening before you found the damage?"

The shopkeeper blinked languidly. "Four young women came in just after ten. They got out of a white limo that parked in the red zone out front. They were sober. The dark-haired one had a bracelet that must have been worth thirty grand—if the stones were real. Pink diamonds. They looked real."

"I see," Mason said, trying to keep his voice even despite his rising excitement. The level of detail that Sargasian was conjuring meant that his mind was intently immersed in his subconscious memory. "Did they buy Billy Blood?" he asked. Maybe one of them had distracted Sargasian at the till while the others painted the six-packs in the display.

"No—two bottles of Veuve Clicquot. I told them they should buy four, so they'd each have one."

"Could they have painted the Billy Blood display?" he asked.

"There's no way they could have hidden a can of spray paint and a stencil under those little dresses. Stripy, flowery, shiny little dresses. Tiny little pocketbooks."

"Good," Mason said. "Did you look at the Billy Blood display after they left?"

Sargasian hesitated. "I walked by it. It wasn't vandalized then."

"So, moving ahead a little, someone else came into the store."

"He was wearing a hoodie, and a little backpack," he said, his gaze unwavering.

"What did he look like?"

"I didn't see his face."

"But it was a guy?"

"He walked like a man. Five-foot-nothing. A gray hoodie and jeans."

"You saw him walk in."

"The phone rang. I had to go into the back. I propped the office door open. From there, I saw him walk in."

"Why did you have to go into the back?" Mason asked. "You have a phone at the register."

"It was my distributor. They had a bunch of questions for me, and I needed to look at the paperwork. The hoodie was looking at the wine display."

"Did you see him leave?"

"No. I talked to the distributor, and the next time I looked, the hoodie was gone."

"Did anyone else come in?"

Sargasian was silent for a minute. "A taxi driver came in and bought a can of green tea. Two cops, two bottles of soda. Then I found the painted cans."

"Could the taxi driver or the cops have done it?"

"No. I was at the register with them. It had to be the hoodie."

"What time was it that the phone rang, and the guy in the hoodie came in?"

"Eleven twenty-one."

"Good," Mason said, surprised at his precision. It was amazing that he had come up with all this, when his conscious mind remembered almost nothing about the evening. Because Sargasian hadn't seen the guy's face, there didn't seem to be anything more to ask him about. Mason didn't want to leave him under for too long either, in case that might have deleterious effects; he'd have to read up on that at some point.

"I want you to close your eyes again," Mason said, "and this time, when you open them, everything will be back to normal. You'll be completely awake. Go ahead—open your eyes."

His eyes flicked open, and he looked disoriented at first, but met Mason's gaze. "What are you grinning at?" he said, irritated.

"You gave me a lot of details," Mason said, and pulled his notepad out of his backpack. He made notes as he repeated to Sargasian what he had revealed.

> distributor phoned at 11:21
> Sargasian took call in office
> perp entered, looking at wine
> gray hoodie, jeans, 5'0"

"I can't believe I remembered all that," Sargasian said. "I guess I can see it now too, but it's fuzzy."

Mason glanced through his notes. "Does your distributor often call you at eleven o'clock at night?"

"Not usually, but it's not unheard of."

"And how did the Billy Blood people get involved? Did you contact them?"

"I called my distributor, I think," he said, frowning, trying to remember. "They must have sent Arko and the camera guy."

"No one ever offered to replace the damaged cans?"

"Oh, god, no. The retailer has to eat that."

Mason nodded, scribbling on his pad. Finally he shoved it into his backpack and stood. "I think we're making progress," he said.

"Keep me in the loop, so I'll know when to sell the painted six-packs," Sargasian said, and followed him back into the shop.

"Is this stuff any good?" Mason asked, pausing at a display of canned espresso.

"Like mother's milk," Sargasian said, gesturing widely, and Mason paid him for two cans.

He put the green bug-eye sunglasses back on and gulped down one of the coffees as he walked toward his bicycle. Sargasian's recall was stunning, but it wasn't a lot of detail to help him identify the vandal. It was a lot more than he'd had yesterday, though, and if nothing else, it would make for good reading in the report for Frey. The hypnosis thing had worked better than he'd thought possible. He smiled to himself. Having a new tool for his work was the best news of all.

While he was in the neighborhood, he wanted to drop by the vandalized billboard. Arko had taken him to a viewpoint several blocks away, but he wanted to get closer. He cycled along the boulevard, keeping his eye on the billboard until he was less than a block away and had to crane his neck to see it. He could see the Billy Blood office a little farther along and across the street, but the roasted-pig party must have broken up, because there was no activity out front. He leaned his bike against a parking meter and stood on the sidewalk, looking up. There wasn't much more to be seen from this angle, except that he could see now that the pink graffiti had definitely been done with spray paint.

On previous cases he'd been able to bleed through to the past to do research—the first time with Laura's help, and later on his own. Both times had been in controlled conditions, but he'd gone back many decades; maybe he could do it again, go back just a few weeks, right here on Sunset.

He looked around, and although lots of vehicles were speeding by on the boulevard, there wasn't any foot traffic. What time of night would a vandal have the best chance of going unnoticed? Long after the bars closed at two, but well before people started going to work, and the workday started early in this town. Three-thirty, he decided.

He moved closer to the parking meter and his bicycle and closed his eyes, clearing his thoughts. He focused on the night Sargasian's store had been hit, and then focused on the time. He remembered Laura's technique, to let information seep in from the fringes of awareness. He tried to keep an image of the billboard and the time in his mind, and anticipate what was just out of reach.

He stood that way for a long time, focusing on that night, trying to render it before him, but it didn't feel like it was happening. Eventually he opened his eyes. Nothing seemed to have changed. Taking a last look at the billboard, he was going to get back on his bike, but then the sky went orange, just for a split second, and then black. He quickly pulled off his sunglasses. It was suddenly quiet—nighttime, he realized. He could see taillights farther down the boulevard, but the midday traffic was gone. The sign on the bank a few blocks away had a display that flashed the temperature, 55, alternating with the time: 3:30. His heart pounded with excitement—he had done it.

He looked up at the billboard, lit from below with a set of spotlights, and saw that it hadn't been vandalized yet. There wasn't anyone up on the scaffolding either. A lone car whizzed by, the driver not even glancing at Mason. Something was slightly off—it looked like nighttime, but it felt a lot warmer than fifty-five degrees. He looked down at his hands, and even though it was night all around him, he was sure he could still feel the afternoon sun on his skin, could almost see it glistening through the dark. He looked away quickly, not wanting to break the spell.

He looked at the bank's clock again, and this

time it read 3:47. He'd been standing here for mere seconds, and seventeen minutes had slipped by. Was he in fast-forward? He looked back down the street, but things seemed to be moving at an ordinary pace. Then something moved in the corner of his visual field—someone was climbing the ladder on the pillar up to the billboard.

Mason could hardly believe what he was seeing. It was exactly the moment he'd aimed for. The guy was wearing a gray hoodie, a baggy backpack, and jeans, and he wasn't very tall. It was the same person who'd hit the liquor store. He was fast—he scrambled up the ladder and looked around, apparently not seeing Mason, peeled off his hoodie, and set to work. How could he have missed him, standing right below with his bicycle? But Mason wasn't really here, he realized, so there was nothing to see. He painted "leave" and "the" in broad strokes of the spray can, then consulted a scrap of paper that he pulled out of his pocket, switched cans in his backpack, and finished the job: "Leave the goats alone." The graffiti didn't obliterate the logo but covered the face of the goat beside it, threads of pink dribbling down the canvas.

He had a sudden thought: his phone. He pulled it out and made sure the flash was off, then zoomed in on the billboard and snapped a picture. The screen was blindingly bright and distracting, so he stuffed it back in his pants.

He was too far away to get a look at the vandal's face, but Mason could tell he was probably in his forties. The guy's T-shirt had a big blocky word printed across the back. Squinting, Mason was able to make it out: INJUSTICIAS. He made a mental note of that, and watched him scramble down the ladder again, hopping onto the roof of the building next to the pillar and disappearing.

"OK," Mason said aloud. "Enough." He hoped this simple act of will would bring him back to the present, ignoring the deeper panic that he might get stuck here. But almost instantly the sky flickered orange again, all around the horizon, and then it was its usual daytime blue. The sudden noise of the traffic was startling, but he laughed out loud and shouted "Yeah!"

He straddled his bike and pulled his notepad out of his backpack, balancing it on top of the parking meter to make notes, still grinning to himself. He wrote down everything he'd seen, including the fact that the guy had referred to a script. That had to mean he was acting for someone else. If he'd thought up the slogan himself, he would have known what words to use. And the word on the guy's shirt—it probably meant "injustice," but there might be nuances that implied something else. Ned would know.

First, though, he had to make another stop: he'd promised Laura that he'd go see Hanh today. Her nail salon was on Sunset too, but much farther east, back in the less gentrified part of Hollywood. He pedaled along with the traffic, feeling energized. Seeing through time to witness the act of vandalism was a major success, and he'd actually been able to switch it on and off at will.

His head hurt, he realized, as he pulled up at the strip mall that housed Pretty Nail Blowout. It wasn't a full-blown migraine, but definitely a headache. It had happened the last time he'd done a bleed-through too, he remembered.

He pulled open the door to the salon and was greeted by the receptionist. A few women sat at nail stations with their manicurists, but Hanh was nowhere in sight.

"Manicure for you today?" the receptionist asked.

"Is Hanh here?" he asked.

"One moment," she said, and picked up the phone, speaking a few words in Vietnamese into the receiver. A familiar petite figure with a sharp wedge haircut soon appeared from the back of the shop.

"I thought it might be you," Hanh said with a smile as she walked up. "The receptionist said there was a river goblin here to see me."

"Am I the only one who thinks that's offensive?" Mason asked, feeling his face reddening. But he was glad to see Hanh relaxed and friendly. The last time they'd met, she'd smacked him across the chops.

"Don't take it so seriously. They never see redheads, especially men." She gestured for him to show her his nails, and he held out both hands for her assessment. "Oh, yeah, you need some work," she said, and turned to walk to a station at the back of the salon. Mason followed, and sat at the little table.

He hadn't really planned on getting a manicure, but it would give him a chance to talk to her.

"Before you get started, do you have any ibuprofen?" he asked.

"Sure." She went toward the back room, calling over her shoulder, "Have you been working today?"

"I have," he said. If she knew about that, she probably knew that Laura had sent him here. It wouldn't surprise him—he knew her powers were remarkable.

She returned with a bottle of ibuprofen and an oversize glass of water. He popped a couple of the tablets and drained the glass, and Hanh set to work on his nails.

"You have the solid fingers of a manual laborer," she said.

"That's not surprising. I'm sure the last fifty generations of my ancestors did exactly that—no princes or pianists that I know of."

She smiled but didn't reply, focusing on his nails.

"So, Hanh, why were you in Los Angeles all those years ago when I wound up there? I was so lost. It was pretty weird to see a familiar face."

"You needed some direction," she said simply.

"Yeah, I think I did. I'm glad I was able to come back."

"With a little help."

"The first time, yes. But I've managed to bleed through a couple of times on my own, and get back on my own."

"Great," she said, and nodded.

"So do you run that doughnut shop all the time ... back then? I don't really understand how that works."

"Things aren't always what they seem," she said.

"That's exactly what Laura said." He watched her for a moment. "It's not really an answer."

"It's more like something you have to figure out yourself," she said, meeting his gaze.

"I keep hearing that too. I just wish it was easier."

"Worthwhile achievements usually involve some work, don't you think?"

"I'm sure that's true." He fell silent for a while and watched her work. "I guess it's just that I feel confident in my abilities when I'm doing the work, and I achieve things using what I know, the psychometry and the minor bleed-throughs. But then I see you and Laura doing things that seem so advanced, moving through time as easily as I walk around my house. It's right at the edge of my understanding."

She grinned at him. "Let me tell you this: you already know reality is malleable, and not everyone experiences it the same way. Time is that way too. The past isn't made of stone, like an office building. It's more like a bouncy house—you know, like at a kid's birthday party?"

He nodded.

"You can think about the past from a distance, with your back turned, like most people do, or you can turn toward it and look at it, the way you did on the street today. You just need to know how to turn and open your eyes. You figured that out on your own."

He wanted to know how she knew he'd had that experience over at the billboard, but he set it aside for now. "What about the time before, when I saw you in the doughnut shop? I wasn't just seeing the past, I was there."

"You were indeed. Like jumping in the bouncy house—you were participating in it. But you have to be careful not to damage the structure."

He watched her work for a few minutes, deftly sculpting his cuticles, while he tried to absorb the concepts.

"I could use your help, Mason," she said finally.

"With what?" he asked.

"I'm having a séance tomorrow evening, and I need another psychic to take part. I have a couple lined up already, but with one more, things should go smoothly. When all the participants are people who flex their psychic muscles regularly, so to speak, we call it a power séance."

The only thing he knew about séances was using a Ouija board, which he'd quit doing because so many sources said it was a religious undertaking to contact spirits and demons, not anything useful or practical for his skill set.

"I have reservations about conjuring the dead," he said. More than being unconvinced that it was a good idea, he wasn't even sure it was possible, akin to trying to undice an onion.

"We're not going to be doing that," she said, frowning. "A séance is meant to achieve the same goals you have in your own psychic work, but with the gestalt of a group. There are all kinds of reasons to hold a séance."

"So what's the reason for yours?"

"We're going to track down a guy who needs finding and help him out. I'll explain the details to everybody tomorrow. You doubt yourself, Mason, but I know you have abilities, and they'll be helpful. What do you say, are you in? There won't be any dead people involved."

Clearly he had no idea what a séance really was— this sounded a lot more exciting. He was intrigued by the idea of participating in a power séance, and he was pleased to be included because of his psychic skills—that was new, being considered legitimate by other people in the field. Plus, Laura had asked him to come here to help out.

"Hell, yes, I'm in," he said. "Let's raise the roof."

She laughed. "It may not get to that point, but I appreciate the enthusiasm."

When she'd finished, he inspected the manicure, which looked flawless. He paid her and headed back out to the street. Before he got on his bike, he checked his phone, and saw there was a text from Ned: "Can Gilbert come over for dinner?"

"Of course," he wrote back. "I'll be home by dinnertime." Gilbert was an old friend of Ned's, and Mason had helped him solve a mystery about his late father's estate when they'd stayed with him out in the Mojave Desert. Mason had always been wary of Gilbert, and didn't completely trust his motivations, but he was getting to know him better and develop some trust. He glanced at the clock on his phone. He still had a few hours to hit the central library, so he pedaled over to the metro station and locked up his bike, then sped downtown far beneath the city's gridlocked rush-hour traffic.

The library was bustling with the after-school crowd, but Mason found an open desk to set up his laptop. He pulled out his notepad and read through what he'd learned today. Most intriguing was the billboard vandal's T-shirt, INJUSTICIAS in big bold letters. Why did that seem familiar? He did a Web search for the word and came up with a myriad of Spanish-language pages, but when he added "Los Angeles" one of the first results was a paid ad for a local law firm, Mangel and Stein. Of course—he'd seen their ads plastered across the backs of buses, on benches, in metro stations. "Personal injury law firm," the English version of the website explained.

He got connected to the library's newspaper archive and dug for articles about Mangel and Stein. There were plenty of news items about the firm's contentious litigation over the years, and he spent some time reading through them. Many of the stories were heavily critical of the firm and its tactics to extract settlements from businesses, and more than one journalist called them "ambulance chasers." That didn't necessarily mean they were scammers; newspapers were big businesses run by big egos, and it made sense they would take the side of other businesses when it came to legal disputes. If the firm really was as toxic as the media made it sound, surely everyone working there would have been disbarred by now.

Whether it was reputable or not, if the firm had commissioned the vandalism, they wouldn't send out an operative wearing their T-shirt. More likely, the guy bought his shirts at a thrift store, like Mason did. The connection between the vandal and the law firm was probably spurious, he decided.

He packed up his computer and his notepad and headed back to the train. It was early evening as he pedaled up the hill to their house, and when he stepped inside he was welcomed by the aroma of cooking.

"Whatever you're doing, it smells amazing," he called into the kitchen, dropping his backpack on the sofa and heading over to the counter.

"White-bean chili and cauliflower tostadas," Ned said, leaning across the counter to kiss him hello. He was still dressed for meetings, dark trousers and a pressed shirt, but wore a red-stained apron over them.

Peggy was working in the kitchen too, ricing the cauliflower with a grater in a big bowl. "I'm calling it the white meal," she said.

"Do you want a coffee?" Ned asked him.

"Sure—set me up," Mason said, sitting on one of

the bar stools. He told them about Frey's speech and its animated atmosphere.

"It sounds like a sales event," Ned said, pouring the pot of espresso into a mug and handing it across to Mason.

"It felt like those IT product launches, with the guy in the turtleneck peddling the new gadget," Mason said. "Frey wore a suit, though."

"You're lucky it wasn't long and drawn out," Peggy said. "I've had to sit through boss speeches that dragged on all day."

"It was short—like twenty minutes. I ducked out before they ate. They had a whole roasted pig."

"Gross," Ned said, wrinkling his nose.

"So does the word *injusticias* mean anything besides 'injustice'?" Mason asked.

"I don't think so," Ned said. "It's kind of a legal term, so maybe it's more specific than the English word. What was the context?"

"This law firm uses it on their bus-bench ads."

"Oh, yeah, I've seen those," Peggy said, looking up from the cauliflower. "Did that come up in your Billy Blood case?"

"It did, but I think it's probably not connected." He told them about hypnotizing the liquor store owner, but left out the part about bleeding through time to watch the vandal; he told them instead that Sargasian had seen the vandal's T-shirt. The less Ned knew about his more far-out activities, the happier they'd both be.

"I can't believe you hypnotized someone," Peggy said. "You've never talked about that before."

"I'd never done it before," Mason said, "but I wanted to try it. I'm really happy that it works."

"When did you learn how?" Ned asked, knitting his eyebrows.

"It's not that difficult. I read some books, and looked it up on the Web."

Ned stared at him. "Did you tell the liquor store guy that?"

"Not exactly," Mason said. "But the point is, it worked, so it doesn't matter how I learned it."

"Isn't that risky, though? You can read all you want about how to do an appendectomy, but I wouldn't want you doing one on me," he said.

Mason shook his head. "It doesn't involve any risk, unless you try to leave something inside the person's head, like 'go knock over a mini mart at three a.m.' But I wouldn't do that." He wasn't actually sure that there was no inherent danger, but he wasn't going to admit that to Ned.

"I hope not," Ned said.

"What happened to supporting my decisions?" Mason demanded, struggling to keep his voice calm.

"That's about your career path, and people paying you because they believe you're psychic," Ned said, moving back to the cutting board, where he was dicing tomatoes. "Hypnotizing people, that's something new."

"You're all about evidence-based beliefs, right?

The evidence is that I pulled memories out of this guy's mind that he didn't even know he had. Those are the cold, hard scientific facts."

"OK, Mason, I get it," Ned said, and sighed. "So will his memories help you figure out who the vandal is?"

"Not really. I think I have to approach it differently, maybe gather more intel on the company, and figure out who has a problem with them. I've ruled out animal rights groups, but maybe there's someone else."

"You said they just became publicly traded," Peggy said. "That means a lot of their internal workings have to be disclosed to potential investors. There should be lots of material available—maybe you'll get some insight there."

"That's a good idea," Mason said.

Peggy looked at Ned and said, "So are you going to tell him?"

"Tell me what?" Mason demanded.

"Don't freak out, but there's something you should see," Ned said.

"Stop telling me not to freak out," Mason snapped. "What's going on?"

Ned wiped his hands on his apron and flipped open his tablet, tapping and swiping at it for a second and then setting it in front of Mason. "More news coverage," he said. "This time, it's national."

Mason felt a surge of adrenaline, making his headache throb. He quickly pressed "play." The report began as a desk story, the talking head with the Billy Blood logo inset over her shoulder.

"The CEO of West Coast lifestyle-beverage maker Billy Blood has employed some unusual means to try to catch the perpetrators of vandalism against his products," she intoned. The story continued with the same interview with Frey that the local news had broadcast, then the same clips of Mason in the liquor store and standing on the sidewalk gawking into space. The caption mangled his name the same way the local station had, "Nelson Wrathway," and identified him as a "psychic consultant."

"At least it was shorter this time," Mason said, draining his coffee and relaxing a little. "And the clips of me didn't look so ridiculous."

"The audience is a lot bigger, though," Ned said. "Potentially millions of people will see that, depending on how many times they run it."

Peggy said dramatically, "As god is my witness, I shall never go hungry again."

"What are you talking about?" Mason asked.

"It's from *Gone with the Wind.*"

"I don't get it."

"I mean that you'll get lots of jobs from all that exposure," she said. "It's like free advertising."

"I don't think I want that kind of client," he said. "People who saw me on TV looking stupid in a liquor store? No thanks."

"Can you afford to be that choosy?" she said gently.

Mason thought about it. "Probably not."

"The upside is that they still spelled your name wrong," Ned said. "Which gives you all the power. People won't be able to find you unless you want them to. You can use it to the max to get new business, and plaster it all over your Web ads. Or you can ignore it—it's up to you."

That was definitely a positive spin on it, Mason realized. Maybe now that the initial shock had worn off, he could consider using the media coverage to support his business.

"I'll have to think about whether my anonymity is worth more than the business leads," he said.

"As far as the media is concerned, it'll be completely forgotten in a couple of days," Ned said. "But you'll still have the video, so you can do whatever you want."

"Thanks for that," he said. "You're both a lot more clear-headed about it than I am right now."

Mason offered to help with the meal preparation, but Ned waved him away, so he grabbed his backpack and went into the office. He felt a flash of guilt when he saw Catherine's briefcase still sitting beside his desk. With all the excitement, he'd completely forgotten to call the car rental place during their business hours. Tomorrow, he thought, and pulled out his phone to put a reminder in his calendar.

He remembered the photo he'd taken of the vandal in action, and pulled it up to examine it. But the image was of the billboard in broad daylight, the blue sky behind it, the pink paint job already completed, no vandal visible. He checked the time stamp; it was for this afternoon, right when he'd been standing on the sidewalk under the sign. He thought about it. Hanh had talked about seeing into the past rather than being there. He hadn't really felt like he was completely there, and if his camera hadn't registered what he'd seen, maybe it was only his mind that had bled through to that night.

He pulled his notepad out of his backpack and flipped through his notes from the day, peeling them off and slipping them into his Billy Blood folder. He read what he'd written about Mangel and Stein, all the negative media coverage. Something felt not quite right about dismissing the connection to the law firm. He pulled up their website again, reading through the self-promoting "About Us" section. "We know how to get things done," it said in summary. "Let us help you fix it." It really did sound shady. He decided to try to intuit whether they were involved somehow in commissioning the vandalism. He closed his eyes and cleared his mind, paying attention to what was drifting around the periphery, as Laura had described. The only image that came to him was the firm's bus ad, with INJUSTICIAS in bold lettering. He let the image go, and thought instead about the vandal. "Who is this guy?" he asked aloud, but all that came to mind was INJUSTICIAS.

Turning back to the computer, he searched for "Billy Blood" and "psychic" to see if any other news outlets had broadcast video of him. The story had been regurgitated a dozen times in written news stories and on blogs, but he couldn't find any new images or footage. That was a relief. He searched for the misspelling of his name, just to be sure, but again found only the original source report and the same string of incorrect replications.

Before long the doorbell rang, and Mason went out to the front room, where Ned was greeting Gilbert. Gilbert gave Mason a tight hug, followed by a wet kiss on the neck. It was just odd enough to unnerve him slightly. Ned would say it was Mason's Anglo uptightness, but Mason had to wonder why Gilbert did things like that.

"It's so good to see you all," Gilbert said, as Peggy came out of the kitchen and gave him a brief hug.

"Sit," Ned said, gesturing to the sofa. "Do you want a coffee?"

"Yeah," Gilbert said, and flopped down on the sofa.

"You look like hell," Ned said as he went into the kitchen.

Mason sat with Gilbert, comfortably far away on the other wing of the sofa, and Peggy went down the hall to her room to change for dinner.

"I'm just tired," Gilbert called to Ned.

"Late nights with Harmony?" Mason asked, grinning. He had introduced Gilbert to his current girlfriend, in return for a favor that she'd done for him in her job as a librarian. To Mason's surprise, it seemed to be working out between them.

"No, man," Gilbert said. "She's in Kansas City with her family for a few days. It's because of the aliens."

"OK," Mason said neutrally. Gilbert was a wide-eyed believer when it came to aliens and flying saucers—but, irritatingly, he was quick to express skepticism of Mason's psychic abilities. "Have you been abducted or something?"

"Not recently," he said. "But they're hanging around my apartment at night, and it keeps me awake. I think I need to get a dog. Dogs freak them out."

"Are they inside your place?" Mason asked.

"No—on the roof, and outside the windows. I haven't seen them, but I hear them."

"Are you sure it's not skunks, or a possum?" Peggy asked, dropping onto the sofa between them.

Gilbert frowned. "Why would you say that, when you saw the alien lights yourself out in the desert?"

"I'm not saying I don't believe you," she said. "But you should eliminate all the other possibilities first."

Gilbert locked eyes with her and raised his eyebrows. "It's aliens," he said firmly.

"Caffeine," Ned said, setting a cup down in front of Gilbert. "Greek-style, with tons of sugar, just the way you like it." He sat nearby in an easy chair.

Gilbert sipped at his coffee and nodded appreciatively. "So I saw you on the news, Mr. Wrathway. You were looking mighty fine."

"Thanks," Mason said. "I'm surprised you watch the news."

"I don't," he said. "Ned sent me a link to the video."

Mason shot Ned a look, but he just shrugged.

"You're on national TV, man. You've made it," Gilbert said.

"That station also plays stories about ax murderers and cute kittens, so I'd say it's a dubious achievement at best," Mason said.

"You're having quite a week, though," Gilbert said. "I heard you totaled a car on the freeway too."

"It was just a fender bender," Mason said. "The worst part is, I wound up with the other driver's briefcase, and I can't seem to track her down."

"What's inside it?" Gilbert asked.

"I have no idea—it's locked. But it's heavy."

"I can get into it for you," he said.

"I'm not going to break into it," Mason said.

"I can get into it without leaving a trace. She'll never know it was opened."

"That's not the point—I don't want to break into it."

"At least show me," he said. "Maybe there's something else we can do."

"Hmm," Mason said, considering for a second. It wouldn't do any harm, he decided. He got up and brought the briefcase and Catherine's other bag from his office, setting them on the coffee table in front of Gilbert.

Gilbert immediately grabbed the shoulder bag

by its bottom and dumped the contents onto the coffee table. He picked up the sweater and unfolded it, ignoring the Billy Blood prospectus. Ned reached over and picked up Catherine's little white notepad.

"This stationery is from the Blue Hills Club," Ned said, riffling through the blank pages. "Maybe that's where she was staying."

"What the hell is the Blue Hills Club?" Mason asked, irritated not by Ned's quick recognition but by the fact that he'd missed something—he hadn't considered what the logo on the notepad meant. How could he have overlooked that?

"It's a golf course for rich people on the Westside. They have tennis and a restaurant too, and some hotel rooms."

"How do you know all that?" Mason asked.

"I work with people who have lots of money," he said. "I've had meetings over there."

"I can tell you that she's from out of town," Gilbert said, holding up the sweater. "Nobody in LA would be wearing this. It's for someplace with snow."

"I already looked into that," Mason said. "She's from Severn, Maryland, and for some reason she rented her car at the vacant airport in San Bernardino."

"She must be NSA," Gilbert said.

"Why would you say that?" Mason asked. But he already knew: Gilbert loved a conspiracy theory, and his understanding of reality was wildly different from everyone else's. He was convinced the Roman Catholic pope had been replaced by a Chinese robot, for example, and then there were the aliens. But one of his conspiracy stories about the banking industry had helped Mason on his first case, so he couldn't dismiss everything Gilbert said.

"It's obvious, man—Severn, em-dee, is where Fort Meade is. And what's at Fort Meade? The NSA."

"I guess that's a possibility," Mason said. "But the NSA can't be the only employer in that town."

"It's more than possible," Gilbert said, his eyes growing wide. "Why would she be out at the dead airport in San Berdoo? Nobody uses that airport—except the military."

"And FedEx," Ned added.

"She didn't get there on a cargo plane," Gilbert said emphatically. "She's NSA. What did she look like, Mason?"

He described Catherine's looks, hair, and clothes as well as he could remember.

"Sounds like a fed to me," Gilbert said. He picked up the briefcase by its handle and felt its weight. "I'm glad you didn't let me break into this. They'd put us all in a deep dark hole somewhere if they ever found out." He set it down again, wiping his hand on his pants. "You can probably just wait for them to stop by and pick it up. I'm sure they'll find it when they want it."

"How could she do that?" Peggy said. "She probably doesn't even know how she lost it."

"I'm sure they've got a tracking beacon in it. Those three-letter agencies don't mess around. They know more about you than you do."

Peggy smiled wanly and looked away. She knew there was no point in arguing with him, Mason realized.

"I'm serious. All the databases are connected—your tax returns, banking records, even when you go shopping—they film you at the register, and that goes in a database."

"Come on," Ned said. "Surely the federal government wouldn't be collecting that kind of information."

"Even if you don't want to believe it, they are," he said. "Have you seen how many cameras there are at the checkout in a big box store? It's all about data collection, baby. Some people say you should only pay in cash, but it doesn't matter—if they have your picture, they can just use facial recognition software to find you in the DMV database, or your passport file."

"You know, she was awfully calm for someone who had just crashed her car," Mason said. "She reminded me of a cop—she had that kind of authoritative presence."

"There you go," Gilbert said. "NSA."

"I'm glad you recognized the logo on the notepad," Mason said to Ned. "I can't believe I didn't try to figure out what it was. I'll call them and see if she's still there."

Ned shook his head. "No way will they ever tell you anything like that. One thing rich people expect is privacy, and at that place, they pay big bucks for it."

"Can I go there?"

"Not through the front gate," Ned said. "I can

probably get one of my banker colleagues to invite you there for lunch—as long as you behave yourself."

"You know I can do that, toots," Mason said, winking at him.

"Oh, yeah," Gilbert said enthusiastically, an idiotic grin on his face. "Go, Mason."

"Do you think the chili is ready?" Peggy asked, catching Ned's eye.

"Absolutely," he said, and jumped up.

The three of them sat at the dining table, and Ned set out bowls of chili and a plate of tostadas before joining them. Gilbert talked about his relationship with Harmony, and Peggy talked about her music. Peggy Pregnant had recently played at a folk festival up the coast, which had given her a chance to connect with a whole new audience. For their last course they had pineapple wedges drizzled with cashew cheese, which Mason ate with gusto once he found that it tasted a lot better than it sounded.

Gilbert said his good-byes a while later, and Mason volunteered to clean up. By the time he'd finished and crawled into bed, Ned had already drifted off. Mason watched him for a minute before he turned out the light, Ned's chest rising and falling with the even rhythm of sleep. He looked so gentle and innocent in the unconscious state, his skepticism and scientific dogma tucked away until tomorrow. It was hard to be upset with him, seeing him like this, Mason thought, and with that his lingering resentment at their earlier squabble evaporated.

As he was slipping into the hypnagogic state, he gave himself the suggestion to be more focused. He couldn't believe he'd missed a significant clue—the logo on Catherine's note paper. "Sharpen up," he said softly.

Vivid images came later in a dream, but he didn't manage to wake up inside it. He found himself standing with Tyler Frey, who was in his impeccable suit, hands behind his back, laughing.

"What?" Frey demanded, glaring at Mason, then laughing more. He pulled his hands from behind his back, and they were dripping with pink paint. He quickly hid them again, his eyes growing round like a recalcitrant nine-year-old, and demanded "What?" before lapsing again into laughter. Mason forced himself awake and found his bedside notepad to write down the details of scene. He wasn't lucid enough to parse it, but he wanted to remember this.

Thursday

The ringing of his cell phone wrenched him awake. It was after nine, but just barely. He pulled it off the nightstand and squinted to see the number. It wasn't anyone he knew, but showed an 818 area code—the Valley. He debated for a second whether to ignore it, but curiosity overcame his grogginess, and he answered, "Braithwaite."

"Good morning," a woman said. "My name is Megan, and I'm calling from LA's number-one mega news source." She recited the call letters.

"Is that a TV station?" he asked, closing his eyes again and pulling the blankets up to his neck. "I've never heard of it."

"Yes, you have," she insisted. "We're number one."

"What do you want, Megan?"

"I'm in the news department, and I have a few questions about your work on the Billy Blood attacks. Have your psychic powers revealed any evidence so far?"

"How did you get this number?" he demanded.

"You're in the book," she said.

"That's a lie," he said, thinking quickly. Cell numbers didn't have a book, and his name had been too garbled in the news coverage for her to have tracked him down based on that. The only way she could have found his phone number was if Frey or Arko had given it to her.

"Anyway," she said, "exactly what kind of techniques are you using in your investigation?"

"I'm not doing any interviews. Don't call this number again," he said, hanging up before she could argue with him. He set his phone back on the nightstand and stretched, staying under the covers.

Frey really was exploiting every possibility to maximize his media coverage. A heads-up about the journalists would have been nice, but they must just assume over at Billy Blood that anyone would be thrilled to be entangled with the media—like being handed a bouquet of flowers, a welcome delight that required no warning. He'd dreamed about Frey last night, he remembered, although he hadn't been able to manipulate the dream. He pulled his notepad off the nightstand and read through what he'd written. He thought about Frey, his demeanor. He'd only spoken to the guy once, and then he'd been handed off to Arko. It made sense, though, that a CEO wouldn't have time to deal with every subcontractor.

What had Peggy said yesterday? Publicly traded companies had to reveal more about their workings than private ones. He wanted to look into that. He steeled himself to face the cold of this absurdly early hour, finally rolling out of bed and quickly pulling on his clothes.

Ned was at his desk, dressed for a home-office day, when he poked his head in.

"Breakfast?" Mason asked.

"I've eaten," Ned said. "You're up early."

"It's crazy, I know. But things are heating up—the circumstances demand sacrifice."

Ned laughed. "You're really going above and beyond, getting up at nine thirty."

"So can you try to get me into Blue Hills? I want to see if I can catch Catherine before she leaves town."

"I know just the guy to ask," he said. "Let me call him."

Mason went into the kitchen and made a pot of espresso, then ate some fruit with it, and made another pot. He took his laptop out on the balcony, still chilly in the cool morning air. For a few hours he sifted through everything he could find about Billy Blood and the company's IPO. A lot of it was financial-industry gobbledygook that probably wouldn't have mattered even if he'd understood it, but he read through it anyway. One document he found listed Billy Blood's legal counsel. There were a lot of firms listed. Mostly they were based in China, but three were in New York, and then, under "West Coast representation," he found Mangel and Stein. He felt the back of his neck prickle, his heart beat faster. He could feel it—he was close.

Why would a big company hire small-time personal injury lawyers? He searched the websites of the New York–based firms that Billy Blood listed. All of them were old-school white-shoe corporate outfits, not a whiff of the slip-and-fall extortionist type among them. But the rules required Billy Blood to disclose all their legal advisers, and for some reason they had done business with Mangel and Stein.

He looked out at the hills of the neighborhood. It still didn't necessarily mean Frey had hired a sketchy law firm to vandalize his own products, but it was an odd coincidence, finding the same firm on both sides of the equation. Mason had done enough metaphysical work to know that what looked like a coincidence on the surface usually wasn't.

Ned opened the French doors and stuck his head out. "Are you up for going over there today?"

"The golf club? Sure," Mason said, folding his laptop closed. Shifting his focus today might help all the details about Billy Blood to percolate.

"My buddy set you up for lunch at one thirty."

"Oh, god—I don't have to eat there, do I? Those upscale places are always all about the meat, and burned-out string beans with cow's butter on them, and iceberg lettuce with boiled eggs and god knows what else. There's never anything to eat."

"You don't have to go to the restaurant," Ned said. "My friend's not actually going to be there. He just put your name on the lunchtime guest list, so you can get in. You'll be on your own."

"Oh … sweet," Mason said, and nodded.

"Just don't break anything, or try to hypnotize people—it'll come back on me. You have to behave."

If Ned hadn't just done him such a huge favor, Mason probably would have taken issue with that, but instead he looked him in the eye and said, "Subtlety, my dear, is one of my greatest skills."

Ned's eyebrows shot up. "Well, you'd better hustle if you're cycling all the way over there," he said, and went back into the house.

"What do I wear?" Mason called after him.

"Business casual," Ned called over his shoulder. "Dark colors."

Before he could get up his phone rang, and when he pulled it out of his pants he saw that it was Arko.

"Hey, man," he answered.

"How's the psychic research going?" Arko asked.

"Great—I think I'm making some progress." It was a vague answer, but Arko hadn't asked for details.

"I wanted to let you know that even though you signed a nondisclosure agreement, it's fine for you to talk to the media about your research," he said. "That was just boilerplate that everybody signs."

He must have heard back from Megan at the

number-one news source, Mason realized.

"But it did ensure that you could film me," Mason said.

"Everybody signs it," Arko said flatly. "But I encourage you to talk to the media when you have the opportunity. It'll help us get to the bottom of this."

It'll also help get Billy Blood in the news, Mason thought, but he said, "I understand, Arko. I'll do interviews if I have time."

"Great," he said, chipper once again, and ended the call.

Mason frowned and stuffed his phone back in his pants. Clearly Billy Blood wanted him to talk to the media, and Arko was almost certainly going to throw more journalists at him. But they should have mentioned this up front.

He went inside, and rooted around until he'd found a presentable shirt and the only pair of dark dressy trousers he owned, dusty from disuse at the bottom of the drawer. He brushed them off and decided not to ask Ned how he looked, since these were the only option anyway. He wrapped a Velcro strap around his right pant cuff to keep it out of his bicycle chain, then lashed Catherine's briefcase and shoulder bag to his rear rack. He rode down the hill and took his wheels on the train, changing lines downtown and riding most of the way to the beach before disembarking, cycling through quiet Westside streets into a gently hilly neighborhood. He found the driveway that led up to the gates of the golf club, and pulled out his phone—he was right on time.

A tall hedge concealed most of what was inside, but he could see verdant manicured fairways and a low-slung building in the distance as he rode up to the gate. The wrought-iron arch above the entrance bore the club's name, Blue Hills, in filigree letters wrapped in stylized grapevines. The effect was less Italian garden and more nineteenth-century textile mill, Mason thought, but it did look expensive, which was surely its primary purpose. He gave his name to the uniformed security guard in the little booth beside the gate, and after a few seconds of typing and staring at his computer screen, the guard nodded.

"You're expected," he said, and the barrier arm over the road swung up.

"Where can I park my bike?" Mason asked.

"Most people come by car," he said. "But some of the staff lock up their bikes outside the kitchen. It's around back, on the left side of the main building."

"Thanks," Mason said, and grinned as he pedaled through the gate. He probably had more in common with the kitchen staff than with the golfers anyway.

He locked up his bike and walked around to the main entrance, Catherine's bags in hand. His pants felt weird, and he realized he was still wearing his cycling strap; he peeled it off and stuffed it in his pocket, hoping he looked more presentable than he had on the national news.

The entrance felt like a hotel lobby, with comfy chairs and sofas spaced around a wide room, and he could see the restaurant off to the left. Even with the lush carpeting and luxe furnishings, it was pretty bland, almost corporate. There were a lot of people floating around, some dressed for golf, some LA casual, others in suits and office garb. He walked over to the restaurant and saw there was a lengthy bar inside too, crowded with boisterous midday drinkers. The dining tables were spaced far apart.

There was a reception counter at the back of the lobby, but rather than asking there about Catherine, he wanted to try Laura's direction-finding technique. He settled into a wing chair at one side of the room and pulled Catherine's bags onto his lap. He closed his eyes, feeling the weight of the briefcase, and tried to expand his awareness. He thought about Catherine, her sweater, the briefcase. Laura had said not to filter the thoughts that came up, but to look to the periphery for the right direction.

It didn't take long—suddenly he simply knew where to go. He wasn't sure how he knew, but he knew she was here. It was a feeling more than an idea in his mind. He stood up and walked into the carpeted corridor that led off the right side of the lobby. These were the guest rooms, he realized, each door with a number, the door handles with key-card readers. He didn't have a room number in mind, just the direction.

He stopped in front of a door marked "Suite B."

His gut told him this was it—Catherine was inside—but the rational part of his mind was still doubtful. His heart was pounding. He took a deep breath, and knocked on the door.

A moment later, a woman pulled it open.

"Catherine Reznik," Mason said.

"You," she said, smiling but looking somewhat perplexed. "The guy in the SUV."

"My name's Mason. I'm so glad you're here," he said. "I've been keeping this stuff for you." He held up her briefcase.

"I wondered what had happened to that," she said. She looked past him, into the hallway, then said, "Come on in."

It was a sitting room, with a sofa and chairs, and a door at the back that led to the bedroom. Mason set the briefcase and the shoulder bag on the coffee table.

"I thought the tow truck driver had it," she said. "I was waiting for him to open it." She gestured to one of the easy chairs and then turned to the built-in bar at the side of the room. "Sit down for a minute. Do you want a drink? I've got bourbon or cheap bourbon."

"I'd better not," Mason said. He'd returned her stuff, and he could easily slip away now. But he was intrigued: what did she mean about waiting for him to open it? He sat down. She came back from the bar and handed him a plastic bottle of water, then sat on the sofa, cradling a lowball glass.

"That must be the good stuff, if you're drinking it neat," he said, twisting the cap off his bottle.

She grinned and held up her tumbler. "Cheers," she said, meeting his eye.

He lifted the bottle and tipped it toward her. "So what do you mean, you were waiting for him to open it?" he asked, glancing at the briefcase.

"The case has a tracking beacon that calls to tell me where it is. But it's only activated when you open it and don't know how to switch it off. You didn't open it, or I would have known—thank you for that."

Mason nodded and took a drink of his water. That wasn't the kind of briefcase accessory you'd get at an office supply store. Maybe Gilbert was right, and she worked for the NSA. Still, there was no reason to be worried, he told himself. "That sounds like a pretty fancy security device," he said.

"It is." She sipped her bourbon and watched him for a moment. "So how did you find me?" she asked, curiosity in her eyes.

"It took a while. I thought you worked for Billy Blood, so I went over to their office, but they'd never heard of you. Finally my boyfriend recognized the Blue Hills logo on your stationery, so here I am. I'm glad you haven't checked out yet."

"Why did you think I worked for Billy Blood?" she asked, watching him closely.

"In your other bag," he said. "The one without the tracking device. It had the notepad from this place, and a prospectus for the Billy Blood stock offering."

"You've put some effort into this. You really are

an investigator."

"How do you know that?" he said, frowning.

"You gave me your business card when we were standing on the freeway, remember? I forgot your name, but the job title stuck in my mind."

"Of course," Mason said, relieved that she hadn't been snooping on him in the tangle of dark databases Gilbert had described.

"But the psychic thing is bull, right? It's just an LA thing to catch people's attention?"

"Actually, it's quite real," Mason said, his cheeks reddening. She wasn't the first skeptic he'd come across, but that didn't make it any less annoying.

"Tell me something psychic, then," she said.

"OK." He set his water bottle on the coffee table and folded his arms. "You work for the NSA."

She watched him for a few seconds. "Exactly who are you?" she asked quietly.

He shouldn't have said that, he realized—and now he knew it was true.

"You've seen my business card," he said, holding up both palms. "That's all there is to it."

"Really," she said, still watching him closely as she took a languorous gulp from her tumbler.

Was just knowing who she worked for a dangerous secret to have? His thoughts flashed to Gilbert's dreaded deep dark hole, a hidden prison for conspiracy theorists and people who knew too much.

"Most psychics say vague things, like 'there's romance in your future,'" she said, still holding his gaze. "Naming my employer, though—that's pretty specific."

She was starting to scare him—he needed to backpedal. "The NSA thing wasn't really psychic," he said quickly. "When I was trying to find you, I saw your phone number on the car rental contract, and the area code was for Severn, Maryland. The number was disconnected, but my friend said that's where the NSA is. And then the James Bond briefcase beacon thing—you have to admit, it's a reasonable guess."

She watched him for a minute, calculating. Finally her eyes softened. "I believe you," she said. "And you're right—it's a pretty good guess."

Mason sighed with relief, then met her gaze again. "So am I right?"

She laughed loudly. "I'm not going to tell you where I work, because it's none of your business. But I do work for the federal government. Lots of people in Maryland do. Satisfied?"

"Completely," Mason said. "I really just wanted to make sure you got your stuff back." He sat forward in the chair, preparing to leave.

She set her tumbler on the coffee table and stood up. "You've gone above and beyond."

"I apologize if I've been nosy," he said, moving toward the door.

"A nosy person would have broken into my case," she said. "You're an investigator. You don't have to apologize for doing what you do."

She thanked him again, and he said good-bye

and stepped into the hall, hearing the door clack shut behind him as he walked back toward the lobby. He took a few deep breaths to try to dispel the haze of adrenaline. She probably wouldn't have done anything even if he hadn't explained himself, but he certainly didn't want to be mistaken for someone who was spying on her, or whatever bogeyman she might have thought him to be. Gilbert was going to love this story.

He walked out of the building and around to his bike, waving to the guard in the little box as he coasted past. He felt relieved, lighter, now that he was rid of that damn briefcase.

An hour later he got home, quickly changing out of his ill-fitting business-casual drag and taking a shower. Ned was on his phone in the office, and Peggy was home from work, sitting out on the balcony, sunglasses on, enjoying the late-afternoon warmth.

He opened the French doors and asked, "Can I join you?"

"Come on out," she said. "I'm just decompressing."

He dropped into a chair and stretched his legs out. "Long workday?"

"Always," she said, and waved her hand dismissively. "Listen, do you want to come and see me perform tomorrow night? I'm going to do the new stuff I've been writing. You haven't heard some of the songs yet."

"I'd love that," he said. "Count me in. Where are you playing?"

"A coffee place on Ventura Boulevard. It's small, and there's no booze, so people can focus on the music. I'll try and rope Ned in too."

"I'm sure he wouldn't miss it." He leaned toward her. "Hey, do you remember Laura, from when we were up at Gilbert's dad's place in the desert?"

"How could I forget? She intentionally out-dressed me."

"Well, I ran into her in Hollywood the other day. We had lunch, and she asked me to go to see Hanh at Pretty Nail Blowout."

"I want to say that's weird, but 'weird' is just a synonym for 'Laura.'"

"So I went to see Hanh, and she invited me to a séance—tonight."

"How cool is that?" she said.

Ned stepped out onto the balcony and stooped down to greet Mason with a kiss, putting his hand on the nape of his neck. "How cool is what?" he asked.

"Mason's going to a séance tonight with your manicurist," Peggy said.

"Seriously?" Ned asked, sitting down with them. "How did that happen?"

"I went by there for a manicure," Mason explained, glancing quickly at Peggy, "and we got talking. She's a psychic too."

"What's the séance for?" he asked.

"I'm not sure yet. But Hanh said it's for psychics

only, so it's sure to be a high-powered one."

Ned was silent for a moment, and then said, "I'm trying to absorb that without saying anything judgmental."

"That's very tolerant of you," Peggy said.

"Your career seems to be"—he sought the right word—"evolving, so quickly. There's a lot of new stuff to wrap my head around."

"You know what a séance is—we've played around with the Ouija board," Mason said. "So it's not really new."

"OK," Ned said, and nodded. "She's not a Spiritualist, is she? They do the séance thing, but they're all about trembling at the feet of the lord. I'd hate to see you get sucked into some cult-y religion."

"It's nothing to do with religion," Mason said. "Hanh's just like me—a practitioner. Only she has a lot more skills. For me it'll be a learning séance. Like driver's ed."

"When do you have to leave?" he asked.

"In an hour or so."

"I'll make dinner before you go, so you won't have to conjure the dead on an empty stomach," he said.

Mason wanted to explain that it wasn't about that, but held back. Ned really was trying, and Mason was going to get dinner out of it; he saw no reason to jeopardize that.

Ned whipped up a lentil curry and some rice, and soon the three of them were at the dining table.

"How did it go at Blue Hills?" Ned asked him,

passing Peggy the bowl of rice. "Did you find the briefcase woman?"

"I did," Mason said, and slapped the tabletop. "She was happy to get her stuff back. And it turns out Gilbert was right—she works for the NSA."

"Did she tell you that?" Ned asked, incredulous.

"Not in so many words, but I asked her if she did, and she didn't deny it."

"I can't believe you asked her," Peggy said.

"I probably shouldn't have," Mason said, "but she didn't seem too upset. I'm just glad I found her, and I don't have to drive that briefcase out to San Bernardino."

"What's going on with the Billy Blood thing?" Peggy asked.

"I looked into their newly public records, like you suggested yesterday," he said. "I found a link between Billy Blood and a shady law firm here in town. Based on what I'd found earlier, it makes me think that the CEO of Billy Blood hired the slip-and-fall lawyers to orchestrate the vandalism."

"Why would he have his own stuff vandalized?" Peggy asked.

"Publicity," Mason said. "You said it yourself— news coverage is free advertising."

"It did make the national news," Ned said. "But that's a pretty underhanded play for a businessperson. You met the guy. Does he seem like the type who'd do something like that?"

Mason nodded. "Oh, yeah. They're entertainment

people as much as they are businesspeople. His speech yesterday was like an old-time revival."

"It would explain the lethargic slogan," Ned said. "'Leave the goats alone.' Any self-respecting animal-rights activist would have used 'Fuck Billy Blood.'"

"Plus, the slogan was painted on the picture of the goat," Mason said. "Someone who was mad at the company would have obscured the product logo."

"Is there any evidence besides the lawyer connection?" Peggy asked.

"No, but it fits everything I've seen. It would explain why they didn't call in the cops—they didn't want to be anywhere near law enforcement. Frey and Arko have both been secretive about the cameras, and then they were nudging me to talk to journalists. They wanted me to it do without telling me they wanted me to do it." He sighed. "In the end, though, if they're responsible for the vandalism, it means I've been duped."

"They used you to get publicity for themselves," Peggy said.

"Even worse," Ned said gently, "they must have believed you'd never get to the truth, or they wouldn't have hired you. It was all for show."

"They hired me to perform like a dancing monkey, not as an investigator," Mason said, pushing his plate away.

"What are you going to do?" Peggy asked.

"First, I'm not going to get upset about being misled. I need to stay levelheaded."

"Excellent," Peggy said emphatically.

"I'm still angry about it, but I'm not going to act on that. And because I did figure it out, that gives me some power—power that they don't know I have."

Ned nodded. "That's the right way to look at it. You're in charge of what happens next."

"I'm not sure if I should go to the cops, though, or just confront the CEO."

"You said he didn't report it to the cops," Ned said.

"No, he never did."

"Then you can't get them involved," Ned said. "If he lied on a police report, sure, bust him. But lying to you and to the media isn't a crime. The cops couldn't do anything with it."

"Good point," Mason said. "I'm going to have to think this through."

He considered asking Ned what he should wear to a séance, but his ego had taken enough of a blow for one afternoon. He pulled on a pair of cargo shorts and a T-shirt, and headed down the hill on his bike. It was dark already. Ever since he'd been run off the road on his last case, biking in the dark had felt somewhat precarious, so he locked up his wheels at a busy corner and waited for the bus.

Hanh's strip mall was quiet. He rapped on the glass door of Pretty Nail Blowout, squaring his shoulders to calm himself. He had no idea what he was in for.

Soon Hanh appeared from the back of the dimly

lit salon, and hurried over to unlock the door.

"Come in," she said. "Everyone else is here." She led him into the back. It was the salon's supply room, he realized, the shelves along one wall stacked with bottles of soap, chemicals, and towels. A desk sat in a corner by the back door. In the center of the room was a round table with five chairs, three of them already occupied by a woman and two men. The men both had gray hair, and one of them was quite elderly. They must have decades more psychic experience than he did, he realized—in comparison he felt like a dilettante.

"This is Mason," Hanh announced. "Mason, this is Anna, and Don Luís, and Mr. Park."

"Hello," Mason said. Hanh ducked back into the front of the shop, so he took the chair between Anna and Don Luís. Mr. Park was looking at him closely across the table, an unflagging happy grin on his face. The lines around his eyes showed that the smile was his default expression, and his bearing was relaxed and confident.

"Do you do martial arts?" Mason asked him.

"A lifetime of aikido," Park said. "You're good."

"It's not a psychic insight. I can just tell," Mason said, and grinned back at him. He'd met people like Park before. They had such advanced manual combat skills that they weren't afraid of much, which gave them a palpable air of calm. They made great party guests, like an anchor that everyone else's insecurities swirled around.

"What kind of psychic work do you do?" Mason asked him.

"For income, I make talismans. I take a client's intention, like passing an exam or getting a promotion, and record it on paper using symbols. If you channel metaphysical energy into the paper during the process, it can be quite effective."

"What kind of symbols?" Mason asked.

"Chinese characters, mostly, in specific styles and arrangements. But in nonrevenue terms, I'm also able to bleed through—as I think we all are," Park said, glancing around the table.

"Are you a commercial psychic?" Anna asked, leaning toward Mason. Her accent sounded Eastern European, and she wore heavy makeup, bright red lipstick that matched her red scarf.

"I guess," Mason said. "I get paid for doing psychic work."

"Do you have a storefront?"

"No," he said. "Do you?"

"Down on Olympic," she said. "I read tarot cards, and palms."

"Do you conjure the dead?" he asked.

"I wish I could," she said matter-of-factly. "Lots of people want to talk to their deceased relatives. I use the cards instead."

"I've never used cards. Is it hard?"

"Yes and no," she said. "It takes a lot of mental energy. I get better insights just going into trance, but clients want a more visual experience. So cards it is."

"That makes sense," Mason said, and made a mental note to read up on tarot cards. He turned to Don Luís and asked, "Are you a commercial psychic too?" but the old man shook his head slightly, uncomprehending.

"He doesn't have much English," Hanh said, returning from the front of the shop, cell phone in hand.

"I'm embarrassed that I live in this bilingual city and only speak one of the languages," Mason said. And to Don Luís, "*Lo siento.*"

Don Luís spoke a few sentences in Spanish, but the only word Mason could pull out was *brujo*.

"You're a *brujo*?" Mason asked. He thought that meant he was a magician, or a witch.

Don Luís nodded.

"It means he's a shaman," Hanh said, "but he has the same skills as us." She took the remaining chair, completing the circle, and spent a moment looking at each of them around the table. Everyone quietly looked back at her. Mason took slow, even breaths to slow his pounding heart. His psychic life had always been intensely personal, not a social experience like this. It was flattering to be included, though, and he hoped he could contribute.

"Thank you all for being here," Hanh began. She set her phone face-up on the tabletop. It displayed a grainy photo.

Mason leaned forward to get a better look. It was a clean-shaven young man with longish brown hair, grinning at the camera. He looked familiar, Mason thought, but he wasn't sure why.

"This is Matt," Hanh explained. "He's supposed to be here-now, but he needs a bit of assistance."

Mason remembered Laura using that phrase, "here-now," meaning where you were supposed to be, your point of origin. There-now, there-then—the terminology quickly got complicated bleeding through time.

"*Comprendo,*" Don Luís said, and tapped the table. Clearly the language gap wasn't a barrier for him.

"The purpose of this gathering," Hanh said, "is to bring him back."

Park nodded confidently, and Anna said, "I see."

Mason hesitated, not wanting to sound incompetent, but he had to ask. "So, where is he?"

"Far," Hanh said, meeting his eye. "Real far. The late eighteenth century. That's why it's going to take all of us to bring him back."

"He got there on his own, but now he's stranded?" Mason asked. That had been his biggest fear when he'd bled through time himself—not being able to come back.

"He stayed too long," Hanh said, and shrugged. "It happens."

"So what's the procedure?" Park asked.

Hanh said, "Palms on the table, focus on Matt, bring him back."

Mason had a dozen questions about how, exactly, he was supposed to help achieve that, but as the others shifted position and moved closer to the table, he decided just to follow along and hope for the best.

Wordlessly, the five of them spread their hands on the tabletop. Mr. Park closed his eyes, his happy grin still plastered on his face, and Anna's head rolled backward, her gaze fixed on the ceiling. Mason glanced at Don Luís, whose eyes had gone glassy, staring into space. Hanh was looking down at the table, but she was breathing deeply, hypnotically. He tried to slow down his breathing too.

He could feel the room changing. At first it was almost as if the lights had dimmed, the shadows in the corners growing deeper, but he knew nothing had physically changed. He started to notice the colors around the room, like seeing flowers blooming that he hadn't noticed before—dark blue bottles of soap, the scuffed white paint on the door, Anna's red scarf. He closed his eyes, and found that he could feel the others, the four of them, warm, glowing like light bulbs. He opened his eyes, and saw that things had changed even more dramatically—everything had taken on more contrast, like a heavily filtered photo.

Hanh met his gaze, and instantly he felt connected to her, knew her feelings, saw inside her mind. That had never happened before, and his rational mind balked. He reasoned that he must just be getting an enhanced reading of her facial expression, or something similarly tangible. But on a deeper level, he knew it was more than that. In this moment he was linked to her, emotionally and without words, linked to all of them. Their collective energy was expanding, filling the room.

Matt, he remembered. He had to focus on Matt. He closed his eyes and brought the photo to the center of his mind, the shaggy guy with the impish grin. In a flash of insight he knew why he looked familiar—he'd had a lucid dream about him, not even a week ago, had met him along a riverbank. At the time he'd thought the guy was homeless, scavenging on the marshy ground, but in context, he must have dressed himself the way people did then. Not homeless, just long ago.

He could feel the dream, connect to it now, with the heightened energy in the room. Matt had been collecting plants, and he'd recognized Mason, asked him for more time. He kept the image in mind, Matt's grubby shirt and stubbly beard, the look in his eyes on the riverbank. He could feel the collective energy coursing through the five of them at the table, and gently directed it into the image of Matt. The others were doing the same thing, he just knew— knew what they were thinking, felt their focus in the shared endeavor.

The tabletop shook under his palms, pulling him out of the dreamy state. When he opened his eyes he recoiled involuntarily, pulling his hands away. Crouched in the center of the table was a man, with matted hair and filthy clothes, his arms covering his face as if fending off a bright light. The pungent, sour smell of homelessness filled the room. The others were still either shocked, as Mason was, or admiring their handiwork.

"Ouch," Park said finally, wrinkling his nose and waving his hand in front of his face.

Was this really their target? Mason could hardly believe they'd done it, and he still wasn't sure they hadn't just conjured a homeless guy from under a bridge. This guy was thinner than he remembered from the dream, and he had a lot more hair. But he moved his arms slowly away from his face, and Mason saw his eyes—it was Matt.

"Ha!" Anna cackled, and stood from her chair. "Victory, my friends, victory." She put a hand on Mason's shoulder, the other on Park's. It felt warm, and meaty, and snapped Mason fully back to awareness. She asked Hanh, "It is the right guy, isn't it?"

"It is," Hanh said quietly. And to Matt, "Are you OK?"

Anna shook with excitement that was transmitted into Mason's shoulder. "He's fine. Just needs a bath."

Hanh stood and put her hands on her hips, concentrating on Matt, who hadn't spoken yet.

"So, can I be on my way?" Anna asked her. "I should get back to work."

Hanh waved in assent, and Anna stepped over to give her an air kiss, then headed toward the back door. "Welcome back, Matt. Good night, all."

Mason couldn't believe she was just leaving, after what they'd achieved. He sat in stunned silence, staring at the grubby traveler. It seemed much more astonishing to have conjured a living person than to conjure the dead. Park stood up and moved back from the table, still observing but distancing himself from the source of the smell.

"Can you stand?" Hanh asked, extending her hand to Matt.

He grabbed it and came down off the table, using her chair as a step, looking unsteady on his feet. Park pushed his chair toward them, and Matt sank into it.

"How long were you gone?" Hanh asked him softly.

He rubbed his forehead, and finally spoke, his voice hoarse. "Six or eight weeks. Maybe longer."

Don Luís said a few words to Matt in Spanish, smiling at him reassuringly. Matt murmured his understanding, and Don Luís rose to leave, nodding good-night to the others.

"You can handle it from here, I think?" Park asked Hanh, touching Matt gently on the shoulder. She nodded assent, and the two men stepped out into the night.

Mason wondered if he should leave too. Maybe it was bad form to hang around after such an undertaking. But he really didn't want to go—he wanted to know if the guy remembered meeting him in his dream, or if that had been Mason's vision alone.

"I thought I was going to be there forever," Matt said, his voice emotional. "Tits-up in the eighteenth century."

"Why did you go?" Mason asked.

Matt looked across the table at Mason. "I remember you," he said. "On the riverbank. You came when I first got there."

Hanh glared at Mason. "Did you trample him?" she demanded.

Mason said, "I don't know what that means."

"He didn't," Matt said. "He just bled through for a minute or two, and I sent him away."

"I didn't do it on purpose," Mason said. "It was just a lucid dream."

"You shouldn't go bugging people when they're traveling," Hanh admonished him.

"It wasn't his doing," Matt said to her. "It was me. I was kind of focusing on him."

"But we'd never met," Mason said.

"You're the Billy Blood psychic," Matt said, looking back at him. "I saw you on TV. I was thinking that I should talk to you, because you were a psychic. That must be what attracted you to the riverbank."

Mason frowned. "But I was just on TV yesterday. I thought you'd been gone for six weeks."

"I was *there* for six weeks," Matt said impatiently, "but I was *here* yesterday."

"OK," Mason said. It was painfully counter-intuitive, but he believed him.

Matt rubbed his temples and looked at Hanh. "It's going to catch up with me, isn't it," he said.

"What is?" Mason asked.

"Remember how you had a headache yesterday

from your bleed-through?" Hanh said, looking at Mason. "It's a physiological side effect. Matt has been much farther away, and for a long time—he will probably get pretty sick."

Mason was about to ask how she knew about his bleed-through yesterday, but Matt interrupted.

"Listen, this is important," he said. "Billy Blood is bad news."

"I've been figuring that out," Mason said. "Their CEO is definitely bad news."

"That's not what I mean," he said. He closed his eyes and rapped his fist against his forehead. "You can't drink that shit."

"I wouldn't," he said. "It's got animal blood in it."

"No one should drink it," Matt said. He closed his eyes again and breathed heavily before he continued. "Do you know what a prion is?"

"Actually, I do," Mason said. He'd often read *Scientific American* as an escape from his office job.

"What's a prion?" Hanh asked. "What are you talking about?"

"It's a molecule that can cause disease by altering your body's proteins," Matt said. "They're dangerous because you can't destroy them by cooking them. Remember mad cow disease? You get that from eating animal brains, but I'm pretty sure there's a different prion in Billy Blood that might really fuck people up."

"From the goat's blood?" Mason asked.

"No—it's one of the plant extracts. I can't imagine why they put it in there, but they do. It's from a plant in the liverwort family. It grows along the LA River—or at least it did in the 1790s. And in China."

"I've never heard of a plant prion infecting people," Mason said. "I thought they were just from animals."

"It was news to me too. But I've studied liverworts my whole career. I'm a researcher at Cal State LA," he explained. "Take my word—it's real."

"Did you bring back samples?" Hanh demanded.

"Yeah," Matt said, patting his hip pocket.

"Then you're going to need to be quarantined," she said.

Matt slumped forward, putting his head in his hands. "Migraine," he whimpered. "Fuck me—it's starting."

Hanh stepped closer and put a hand on his shoulder, seemingly oblivious to the stench radiating from him.

"So how did we bring him back?" Mason asked her quietly. "It worked, which is amazing, but how?"

She scowled at him. "Mason, I've got other priorities right now."

Matt moaned, his pain clearly getting worse.

"I've got to get him settled," she said, and gestured toward the back door with her thumb. "Would you mind?"

"OK," Mason said, rising from his chair. "Do you need a hand with him?"

"No. Just go." As he walked to the door, softening her tone, she said, "Thanks for helping out. You did great."

"Call me if you need me," he said, and closed the door behind him.

On his walk back around the end of the building to the boulevard, he was high on adrenaline—Hanh had said he'd done great, which had to mean he'd pulled his own weight in there. It was energizing, unleashing that kind of power. With all this psychic work, he mostly felt like he had no idea what the hell was going on, but still, he was *doing* it—achieving things, getting answers, even holding his own in a group of pros.

What was she going to do with Matt, though? There wasn't even room for a cot in her storeroom, much less room to set up a quarantine. What that guy needed was a long shower and a dose of morphine.

He sat by the window on the bus and watched the dark streets roll by, digesting everything that happened and breathing deeply to get calmer, dispel the excitement. The lucid dream about visiting Matt on the riverbank had been a real experience, shared with the guy—was that why he'd been asked to help out with the séance? The more he thought about it, the more he knew it couldn't be a coincidence. As Laura said, there are no coincidences. Matt had wanted to tell him something about Billy Blood, and claimed he'd brought Mason to the riverbank, but in the dream he'd quickly sent Mason away. Maybe he'd somehow summoned him to the séance too.

And what was he supposed to do with the allegation that Billy Blood was putting people's health at risk? He wasn't even sure it was credible; Matt had been a complete mess, emotionally undone. If it was real, it was something for Matt to deal with himself, he decided. He had enough Billy Blood trouble of his own. Ned was right that he couldn't go to the cops, and if he talked to a journalist, he ran the risk of getting sued for breaking the nondisclosure contract he'd signed. Ideally he'd get paid first, and then the truth could come out. But all he had was his instinct that Billy Blood Corp was somehow more involved than it appeared. Without solid evidence, who would even believe him? First, though, Frey wanted a written report, so he was going to have to come up with a plan.

When he came into the house, Peggy was stretched out on the sofa, wearing her headphones, but she pulled them off when she saw Mason.

"Where's Nedly?" he asked her.

"He went to bed," she said. "How was your séance?"

"Pretty damn amazing," he said quietly. "I'll tell you all about it, but is there anything to eat? I'm famished."

"I made hummus earlier, if you want that. There's some of those mini peppers to eat it with."

"Hallelujah," Mason said, and went into the kitchen, digging around in the fridge.

She came over and sat on a barstool at the counter, and between bites he told her what had happened at Hanh's salon.

"I can't believe that's even possible," she said. "Dragging someone through time? It's nuts."

"I don't think we could have done it for someone who belonged there," he said. "When you bleed through like he did, it's almost like you're not completely there. You're still anchored here, and you can be pulled back."

"It's freaky, Mason, but I love that you're doing this stuff. Are the other psychics the kind of people you'd hang out with?"

He thought about it, crunching on a pepper. "I don't think so. The only thing we have in common is the psychic power. One of them runs a fortune-telling shop, and another one is all about martial arts. I guess I'd consider them colleagues. It's like the people at your firm—how many of them would you want to hang out with after work?"

"Not many."

She gave him a little congratulatory hug before she went back to her music, and Mason went into the bedroom, where Ned was still awake, reading a novel.

"How did it go?" he asked, putting the book facedown on his belly.

"Pretty great," Mason said, peeling off his clothes and climbing into bed. "We were able to contact the person we were targeting."

"Through the Ouija board?" Ned asked, looking dubious.

"We used a different method," Mason said vaguely. "But it worked out really well." Rather than explaining what they'd done, he told Ned about the other participants—Anna with her storefront, Mr. Park, and Don Luís.

"They sound like interesting people," Ned said.

"Big time," Mason said, and kissed him goodnight. He felt conflicted about not sharing the whole truth with Ned, but the less he said, the less he had to defend. It was becoming a pattern, a habit, the path of least resistance. Anyway, Ned seemed happier not knowing all the details. They didn't have to share absolutely everything, he reasoned, and in his heart Mason knew they would never agree on this stuff.

He was exhausted, he realized, despite feeling amped up from the evening's excitement, and quickly drifted into the hypnagogic state. He wondered if he'd maxed out his psychic circuits, because he didn't dream about anything that he could remember—he found only deep, restful sleep.

Friday

nce again Mason awoke to his ringing phone. "Damn it," he said, scrabbling on the nightstand for it. He was going to have to start leaving it on silent until he woke up.

He didn't recognize the number, but it was local, and he picked up. "Braithwaite," he snapped.

"Hello, Mr. Braithwaite," a man's voice said. "I'm calling from *Va-Voom Los Angeles*. I wondered if you might have a few minutes to chat."

He knew the newspaper, and despite being the city's biggest source of classified ads for escort services, they also did some serious journalism. But he wasn't about to help publicize Billy Blood's fake victimhood.

"Tell Frey he can do his own interviews," Mason said.

"Frey? The CEO?" he said. "That's not where I got your number. A friend of mine, Gilbert Quintero, told me that he knew the Billy Blood psychic. That's you, right?"

"Who is this?" Mason asked.

"My name is Danny Santos, and I write freelance for *Va-Voom.*"

"You're a friend of Gilbert's?" he asked, rubbing sleep out of his eyes. Trust Gilbert to spill the beans. "Can you get him a job? He seems to have too much free time."

"Ha," Danny said. "So how did you first meet Tyler Frey?"

"No," Mason said, "we're not doing that. Talk to Frey, or Arko Ramsey—he does their PR."

"But you're the one with the interesting angle," Danny protested. "The psychic thing. People eat that up."

"It's nothing personal," Mason said, "but I'm not going to talk about it. Say hello to Gilbert." He hung up before Danny could say anything else.

He decided not to go back to sleep, and dragged himself out of bed to make coffee. Ned was already out at meetings, and the house was quiet. After a couple of cups of espresso and a bowl of berries, he started to wake up, and took his laptop and coffee mug out onto the balcony.

He wanted to broaden his research on Billy Blood.

If Frey had indeed orchestrated his own vandalism, there might be more chicanery to be found in his past. He spent a couple of hours reading about the genesis of the company, and then about the CEO's personal history. Before Billy Blood, Frey had worked in ad sales for a string of businesses, including a local TV station, which made sense: he would have connections to help him wrangle the week's news coverage.

Nothing he found implied that Frey had been a fraudster in his past life, but there was a lot of gray area between acting unethically and acting illegally. Eventually he set his laptop aside and stretched out in his chair. Maybe there was a better way to get a sense of it.

He closed his eyes and cleared his mind, thinking about Frey, and then the Billy Blood logo. It was such a loud design, so garish. The image started to shrink, slowly receding into the distance, until finally it was just a bright yellow speck in the nothingness. There were other bright dots around it, not fixed like the stars but moving, dipping and waving, more like fireflies in the forest, or plankton in the sea.

He opened his eyes and sighed. It wasn't an especially helpful image, but he wrote it down anyway. Then he spent some time looking at the news online, first searching for the garbled version of his name, and then his real name, to make sure there was no new coverage floating around with his face in it. But there were only derivations of the national story and the original piece done by Frey's cronies in the local news.

His phone rang in his pants pocket. "Not again," he said as he pulled it out. It was Arko's number. He had no desire to talk to the guy, but he did want to get paid, so he picked up.

"Hey, Mason," Arko said. "I was hoping to touch base about your research today. How's it going?"

"Quite well, actually. I may have some answers for you."

"Oh, really? What did you learn?"

"I'll put it all in my written report," Mason hedged. He had no idea if Arko was in on the skullduggery at Billy Blood, but either way, he wasn't about to take him into his confidence. "I'm working on it today, and I thought I might drop it by tomorrow or Monday."

"I'm sure that'll work fine," Arko said, but he sounded doubtful.

"Thanks, Arko—I'll be in touch." He ended the call and stuffed his phone back in his pants.

He wasn't ready to write up his findings for Frey. He thought he knew what had happened, but it was all unsubstantiated. Presenting that to Frey in writing was just asking for trouble.

Moments later the phone rang again.

"Come on," he snapped, and fished it out of his pants. The screen said the call was from "Blue Hills GC." He answered and heard Catherine's voice.

"I wanted to thank you again for bringing over my briefcase. It saved me a lot of paperwork," she said.

"I'm glad I finally found you," Mason said, and

waited for her to continue—another thank-you couldn't have been the only reason she'd called.

"Also, I wondered if you might be able to drop by here again."

"Am I in trouble?" Mason asked, feeling his heart pounding.

She laughed. "No, nothing like that. I just have some information that I think you'll find useful. I promise you'll be glad you came."

He considered that. It was intriguing to be summoned this way, and it didn't seem like he had any reason to be afraid of her. "OK—I can do that." Looking at the clock on his computer, he said, "Are you around this afternoon?"

"Yes—come on over."

"I'll be there in an hour or two," he said, and ended the call.

It had to be about Billy Blood—besides the car crash, Billy Blood was the only overlap he had with her. She had the company's prospectus in her bag, and he was very publicly working for them. To placate his nagging doubt, he sent Ned a quick email explaining where he was going and why.

He changed into clothes that wouldn't make him stand out at Blue Hills—a pair of chinos and a collared shirt—and pulled on his backpack, then wheeled his bike out of the garage and coasted down the hill. Soon he was aboard the train, headed to the Westside. Once he was there, he cycled through the leafy neighborhood to the entrance to Blue Hills, stopping at the guard's booth.

"I have a meeting with Catherine Reznik," he said, hoping she'd left his name at the gate. Sure enough, the barrier arm swung up, and he continued inside. He locked up his bicycle outside the kitchen, then walked around through the front door.

The place was busy, full of golfers and business-people. Mason strode through the lobby into the lodging wing. There was no answer when he knocked on Catherine's door; he tried again, then walked back to the lobby. He remembered that she was a drinker, and the restaurant had a full bar.

He scanned the crowded room, and there she was, the familiar blond haircut, perched on a stool at the far end of the bar, a tumbler in hand. She seemed lost in thought, but then she looked over and saw Mason in the doorway, and quickly stepped off the stool. She was so not an Angeleno, he thought, watching her walk toward him. She was dressed in a utilitarian office top and dark slacks, her style all about blending in, not attracting attention.

"Thanks for coming," she said, standing in front of him. He felt her assessing him anew, searching his face for something. "And pardon my lack of transparency on the phone."

"I must admit, you've piqued my curiosity."

"Come on back to my suite, and we'll talk."

The bartender looked over at them curiously as they left. Mason followed her, relieved that so many people were seeing them together. If he did get spirited away, at least Ned would be able to find witnesses.

Mason stood near the chair he'd occupied yesterday, and Catherine returned to the bar, sloshing some bourbon into a glass.

"I'm starting chapter two here," she said. "No booze for you? Are you in AA or something?"

"I'm afraid it'll clog up my aura," Mason replied. He wasn't really worried about that, but it was a such a great line to toss at a skeptic. He did want to earn her confidence, though, so he said, "Why not—I'll join you."

"Neat, or on ice?" she asked.

"Neat if it's the good stuff, and ice if it's not," he said.

She chuckled and came back to the sitting area, handing him a tumbler and dropping onto the sofa. Mason sat down too, and she tipped her glass at him and said, "Cheers."

He took a tiny sip; he couldn't tell what brand it was, but she'd brought it without ice, and the initial gentle burn was delicious.

"So," she said, her tone becoming businesslike, "I know you're the psychic for Billy Blood. I believed you yesterday when you said that pegging me as NSA was just a good guess, but in my business we verify everything, so I looked into you."

"That sounds ominous," Mason said, shifting uncomfortably in his chair.

"It's not. If you don't have anything to hide, you have nothing to worry about."

"OK, that sounds even more ominous."

She smiled. "I've been doing some research on Billy Blood. I know that you've only been involved with them for a short time."

"I went there looking for you on Monday," he said. "That's the first I'd ever heard of Billy Blood. I met the CEO, and he hired me to look into the vandalism of his billboard and his products at some local shops." Even though he didn't need to tell her all that, he felt safer being completely up-front, considering the scale and power of the entity she represented.

"You dealt directly with Frey?" she said. "I'm surprised. He's a busy man."

"I was carrying the prospectus when I walked in there, so they thought I was going to buy in. I got the red-carpet treatment until they figured out what was happening."

"Ah. That explains it." She nodded. "He's all about the people with the money. That's why I'm here—Frey plays golf at Blue Hills, usually with potential investors, and that's who I am this week."

"You're posing as an investor?" he asked.

"I'm not posing. That's who I am," she said, a glint in her eye.

"OK," he said. Clearly she was sticking to her cover story. "Have you been able to golf with him?"

"A couple of times."

"Why are you researching Billy Blood?"

She watched him for a second, then said, "My impression is that you're not in on what's going on at

Billy Blood. You're more of an outside contractor. Is that accurate?"

"Do you mean Frey arranging for his own vandalism and then crying victim in the media? I'm not in on that, but I figured it out."

Her eyebrows shot up. "That's the conclusion I've reached as well. Props to you for uncovering that."

"I know what I'm doing," he said, frowning and taking a slug of bourbon. He didn't need her congratulations; he'd be more flattered if she hadn't been surprised that he was competent at his job.

He met her eye. "When they brought me in, I thought it was to do legitimate research, to find out who the vandal was. But everything points to Frey setting it up through Mangel and Stein. I was never really supposed to identify a culprit—Frey is probably as big a disbeliever as you are. I was hired to perform for their cameras and attract media attention, but no one told me that. I figured it out on my own."

She nodded. "That rings true."

"Is that why you called me here, to tell me that I'm Frey's dupe? Because I already knew," he said.

"That was part of it, but there's more." She took a sip of her bourbon. "You seem to be skilled at deductive reasoning, Mason. Can you imagine why the government might be interested in Billy Blood and their connection to Mangel and Stein?"

He thought for a minute. "Probably because Frey used the word 'terror' in an interview with the *Charlotte Scoop & Analyzer*. It's an establishment paper, and I'm sure that word makes you people prick up your ears."

She smiled. "Very good. I'd like you to take a look at a couple of documents. Do you have a computer with you, or your cell phone?"

"I have my laptop," he said.

"Open it up, and type in this Web address."

Mason dutifully pulled his laptop out of his backpack and set it on the coffee table, moving his tumbler out of the way. Once he was online, he looked up at Catherine and said, "OK—fire away."

She had pulled out her cell phone and read him a string of letters and numbers. It didn't seem like a web address, but finally she got to a domain, .AH, which he'd never seen before. It brought up a blank page with an empty box at the top. "This goes in the input field," she said, and read another string of digits. When he'd typed it all and hit "enter," a document started downloading.

"Don't misplace that," she said. "Once it's finished, the link and the server will disappear."

Mason clicked it open; it was thirty-six pages long.

"What is this?" he asked.

"Read through it—you'll figure it out. I've got a couple of calls to make. I'll be in the next room." She went through the doorway into the bedroom, leaving the door ajar.

The first page in the document was a screen shot of an email to someone named Mike Valdez at Mangel and Stein. It had been sent from a nondescript email address without the sender's name, but it was signed "Tyler."

"Per our discussion," it began, "I think pink is the best color to use. It will contrast nicely with our logo."

"My god," Mason said under his breath. Catherine had hacked into Frey's email.

The next page was labeled "Transcript," presumably of a phone call, because two phone numbers were listed below that, one with "Tyler Frey" written after it in brackets, the other marked "Mangel and Stein switchboard." Mason read through the conversation. The juiciest part appeared three-quarters of the way down the page.

"Hit the billboard on Sunset," Frey had said. "It's highly visible, and it's near my office. That'll get everyone's attention."

Mason read quickly through several more phone transcripts, one between Mike Valdez at Mangel and Stein and Hector, the guy who had climbed the billboard, with Valdez dictating exactly what words the vandal should paint, encouraging him to write it down so he'd remember.

It was damning evidence, and a lot of people had been surveilled to gather it—half a dozen email accounts, and as many phone numbers. Catherine and her people were not messing around. He felt a flutter in the pit of his stomach. Gilbert was right again: our right to privacy was an illusion in the face of this kind of power.

He could overhear Catherine on the phone in the next room.

"Can you get me out tonight?" she said. "No, you won't find my outbound, because I came on a transport…. Yeah, a red-eye is fine, as long as I'm in first."

She was leaving tonight. He read through the rest of the emails and transcripts, then quickly added a password to the file. It wasn't much of a security measure, but at least it wouldn't be casually exposed if someone used his computer. He sat back in his chair to absorb it all. He'd been right about everything. Annoyingly, so had Gilbert.

Catherine came out of the bedroom and sat on the sofa again.

"Why have you given me all this?" he asked.

"It's just a little help," she said. "You could have uncovered all this yourself if you'd kept at it a bit longer. You were most of the way there."

"I might have been able to sneak a look over Frey's shoulder at his email or something," he said, "but retroactively tapping a law firm's phone lines? I don't think so. What am I supposed to do with this?"

"You worked in journalism," she said. "I'm sure you still have contacts who are good at protecting their sources."

"The journalists I knew covered red-carpet events, and chased after celebrities outside restaurants. What am I going to tell them? 'Here's some stuff I got from the NSA?'"

She looked appalled. "Mason, you're smarter than that. It could have come from any number of people inside Billy Blood, or at the law firm. Leave me out of it."

He thought for a moment. Of course he couldn't tell anyone where he'd obtained this. "So you want it to see the light of day," he said.

"Terrorism had nothing to do with anything that happened at Billy Blood," she said. "Frey deployed an underhanded marketing tactic, which doesn't concern me, but he shouldn't have touched that word, 'terror.' It's been a complete waste of my time, and considerably expensive."

"Yeah, I thought the whole terrorism thing was hyperbole from the get-go," Mason said.

"We live in an era when the wisdom of the market is considered paramount," she said, picking up her tumbler from the coffee table. "I'd love to see what the market does with that information. It might get expensive for someone other than the taxpayer for a change."

"But what about the risk to me?" Mason said. "I don't want Frey suing me."

"Why would he think it came from you?" she asked. "Set the information free, but do it carefully. He'll have bigger problems than worrying about you. You'll be fine."

That was easy for her to say, he thought. But he knew she was right. It was theoretically possible not to be implicated.

"Why don't you just send this to a journalist yourself?" he asked.

"I can't take that kind of risk," she said. "And you already have those contacts, don't you?"

"Probably," he said, and picked up his tumbler, draining it and feeling it burn in his throat. "What if I don't release it? Delete the file, forget I ever saw it?"

She looked away. "You can do whatever you want," she said, waving her hand dismissively. "I just thought you and I might be on the same page. Frey has wasted my time, and he's played you."

"That is infuriating," Mason admitted. "Still, I'm getting paid."

"As well you should. But he hired you to find out who vandalized his stuff. Technically, releasing those documents is exactly what he's paying you to do." She stood and smoothed the front of her slacks. "Listen, Mason, I'm sure you'll make the right decision. I've got to get on a plane in a few hours."

"Are you flying out of San Bernardino again?" he asked, folding his computer closed and stuffing it into his backpack.

Her eyes grew wide. "Aren't you the thorough researcher," she said. "You should come work for us."

"Hell, no," he said firmly, standing up and slinging his backpack over his shoulder. And more gently, "It was on your rental contract that day—you rented your car out by the San Bernardino airport."

"Got it," she said, and smiled as she led him to the door.

"Can I get your number or email?" he asked her. "I just realized I have no way to contact you."

"No," she said. "There's no reason for you to have my contact info."

"But what if I need to talk to you about all this?"

"You won't," she said with a faint smile, and pulled open the door. "Take care of yourself, investigator."

"I'll try," he said, and stepped out into the hall.

He felt a little dazed as he unlocked his bike and pedaled down the driveway, and not just from the warm glow from Catherine's bourbon. Witnessing the reach of her research abilities was like the effect the car crash had on him the day he first met her—it was unsettling, like the world had shifted and things didn't work the same anymore. Breaking into someone's email wasn't that shocking, but she had phone transcripts from conversations that had taken place well before the billboard had been vandalized, when Billy Blood would have appeared on her radar. That meant those phone calls had been recorded proactively. Maybe everyone's phone calls were being recorded. Was Gilbert right, that the three-letter agencies knew way too much about everyone? It was worrying to consider that everything he understood about the world might be a false construction.

"I got your email earlier," Ned called to him from the kitchen when he walked in. "You don't usually send me your schedule."

"I was meeting the NSA woman, and I was worried about disappearing," he said, dropping his backpack on the sofa and taking a stool at the kitchen counter. "Getting thrown in one of the secret prisons Gilbert talked about."

Ned laughed. "Since when is Gilbert your primary source of factual information?" He was chopping up a head of broccoli.

"I'm going to be listening to him a lot more carefully from now on. So many crazy things he said turned out to be true."

"Really? What happened?"

"It turns out she was investigating Billy Blood, just like I was. You can't tell the media you're a victim of terrorism without attracting the attention of the government. She gave me some documents that prove Frey hired someone to vandalize his own billboard."

"Really?" he said, looking up, his knife pausing in mid-cut. "Why would she do that?"

"She wants me to release it. She's annoyed with Frey for wasting her time, and she knows he played me. She assumed I'd want to out him."

"That makes sense," he said.

"But isn't she playing me too by having me do her dirty work? I'm not sure it's worth the risk to me."

"That's up to you, but you'd be doing the world a favor by making that guy look bad."

"Are you making dinner?" Mason asked. "Isn't it a bit early?"

"We're going to see Peggy perform tonight,

remember? I figured you wouldn't want to wait until afterward to eat."

"I completely forgot. It's been a weird day."

He changed clothes while Ned stir-fried the broccoli with some garlic and red peppers, and after they'd eaten Ned backed the Barracuda out of the garage, and Mason jumped in the passenger seat. The venue Peggy was playing was in the Valley, not all that far away, but they got caught in commuter traffic on the freeway.

"Why doesn't this woman just go to the media herself?" Ned asked, keeping his eyes on the car in front of him.

"I asked her that, and she said it was too risky for her. Plus I actually think she wanted to help me out. Anyway, she's on her way back to DC tonight."

Ned parked on a side street a couple of blocks from the coffeehouse, and when they walked in Peggy was already sitting on a stool on the little stage, her long straight hair wrapped in her daisy headband, cradling her acoustic guitar in front of her massive faux belly. Half a dozen patrons sat around at the tables, some of them clearly waiting to hear from Peggy Pregnant and others just there to drink coffee, but Ned and Mason were able to find chairs facing her. It was a modest performance space, but even so, someone switched on a spotlight, illuminating her glorious folky persona. She adjusted the mike, pulling it toward her, before she began.

"My name is Peggy Pregnant," she said, "and I

want to thank you for being here tonight." There was a smattering of polite applause. "I'm going to do a couple of new songs, if this little rascal will let me," she said, massaging her belly.

The woman sitting in front of Mason leaned over the man beside her and asked quietly, "Is she actually pregnant?"

"I don't think so," the man said. "I'm sure I saw her at a folk fest, like, three months ago, and she looked exactly the same. She was drinking Jim Beam straight out of the bottle. I don't think a pregnant woman would do that."

Ned stifled a laugh and exchanged looks with Mason.

Peggy launched into her first song, strumming her guitar. It had a bright, upbeat melody, and she played the intro with confidence, filling the room, and eventually adding her voice.

> I picked you because you're a mild one, darlin'
> Not really a wild one
> Don't know where you came from
> But your time with me has just begun.

There were a couple of verses, and an instrumental stretch, and when she finished, the crowd clapped and hooted.

"She's still got it," Ned said.

Peggy played four more songs, only a couple of which they'd heard before, and then took an awkward bow, exaggerating the difficulty she had in maneuvering while extremely pregnant. Mason went up to the counter and bought an espresso to go, and they watched Peggy spend a few minutes glad-handing her audience, but they left without talking to her. They'd see her at home. They chatted about the show as they walked back to the car, and made it home without traffic.

"We have some episodes of *Pica Confessions* that we haven't watched," Ned said when they walked into the house. "I saw a preview: one of them is this woman who eats sofa cushions, and she confesses to her mom at a wedding. 'Mom, I eat sofa cushions.' TV doesn't get much better than that."

"As amazing as that sounds, I think I'm going to do some work. Billy Blood isn't going to pay me unless I write them a report."

Ned went to watch TV, and Mason set up his laptop on his desk in the office. He knew exactly what to write. Catherine had made that part easy. He didn't have to worry about making groundless accusations—he knew it was all true—and he intended to lay it out clearly. The trick was to do that without revealing that he'd had it confirmed with email hacking and wiretaps. Frey would almost certainly shred the report, but at least he'd see that Mason wasn't going to play the patsy as he'd planned. He wasn't going to wait until Monday, either—he was going to present this to him at the earliest opportunity, so he could stay on top of it. If the story came out before Mason talked to him, Frey would assume he'd lifted the details from the media. He wanted the satisfaction of throwing this in Frey's face himself.

He wrote it in the third person, so it read like Mason had some distance from the facts. It didn't take long to describe the past week: the meeting with Arko and the trip to the liquor store, the details that had come out of the hypnosis session with Sargasian, the news coverage. He left the part about Mangel and Stein until the last few paragraphs, trying to write in objective language.

> CEO Frey conspired with Mike Valdez of Mangel and Stein in planning the vandalism. Frey directed Valdez to select the billboard on Sunset Boulevard for the initial act of vandalism, citing to Valdez its advantageous visibility and proximity to the Billy Blood corporate offices. Frey also instructed Valdez to use pink paint for the vandalism, as pink would contrast effectively with the Billy Blood product logo. Valdez or another staffer at Mangel and Stein devised the phrase to be inscribed: "Leave the goats alone." Valdez directed Hector Gutiérrez, the individual contracted to carry out the vandalism on billboards and on product displays at liquor stores, to record the phrase on paper so as to be able to reproduce it correctly.

He wondered whether he should add something about the toxic prions Matt has told him about. It was really tangential to what he'd been hired to do, and Matt hadn't been all that convincing. He decided to let it go.

He saved the report but didn't print it yet. He'd double-check it tomorrow. By the time he climbed into bed, Ned was already asleep, but he mumbled something sweet sounding as Mason switched off the light.

Too many words, he thought, drifting toward sleep. They were swirling around in his head. Soon he found himself walking on a dark street in a warehouse district. It looked like parts of Rio Bosque, a rough industrial town where he'd done a job not long ago. He struggled to become aware inside the dream but couldn't quite get there. He knew, though, why he was there: he was looking for Tyler Frey. The guy was out here somewhere, hiding in a dark corner. Flickering light spread around him, reflecting on the walls and the grimy street, but there was no one in sight. The light came from a primitive torch Mason was carrying, he realized, looking at it in his hand. It was burning at the top, a crude light source for the unlit streets. The glare made it hard to see anything else when he looked at it, but things were clearer when he held it higher, above his line of sight.

Saturday

The alarm went off early, and Mason sat up on the side of the bed so that he wouldn't fall back asleep after he switched it off. He wasn't quite ready to embrace the morning the way Ned did, but he had his regular appointment today with his shrink, Miss Cassie, and she seemed intent on getting him into her office as early as possible. He suspected it was a tactic to force him to get up early, but he let it slide; he had to pick his battles with her.

He went to the kitchen, on the way poking his head out the French doors to say hi to Ned, who was sitting in the cool morning air reading the news. He started the espresso machine, munching on some fruit and muesli, slowly coming alive as the caffeine sank in. Eventually he felt functional enough to look at what he'd written last night, and went to his desk.

Overall the report read well, and needed just a couple of tweaks. When he was satisfied with it, he sent it to the printer, then pulled out his phone and dialed the number Frey had given him. He could feel his heart beating faster. Arko answered, cheery as always.

"Hey, Arko," Mason said. "I'd like to talk to Frey, if you could put him on."

"He's not in the office, and neither am I. It's Saturday."

"I can't believe the CEO of a billion-dollar company takes Saturday off. And you answered your work line."

"I can't disturb him today. Is it something urgent?"

"I'd like to submit my report. Can you have him call me?"

"I'd be happy to take your report, and pay you," Arko said. "But it'll have to wait until next week."

"I can wait a few days—no problem. But I want to talk to Frey myself. Tell him I know exactly who vandalized your stuff."

"Who was it?" Arko asked, his voice rising.

"I'll explain that to your boss. You could mention the name Mike Valdez."

"Is that the perp?"

"No. Just tell Frey that I know about Valdez."

"Let me get a pen," he said, and then asked Mason to repeat the name. "I don't see why you can't just tell me what's going on," he said, sounding miffed.

The fact that Arko didn't recognize Valdez implied that he wasn't in on the deception at Billy Blood. None of Catherine's documentation had mentioned Arko either. Even so, Mason wasn't going to spell it out for him.

"It's nothing personal, Arko. It has to be Frey."

He ended the call and got ready to leave, carefully putting his report for Frey into a blank file folder and slipping it into his backpack, in case it came up sooner than next week—as he knew it would. He kissed Ned good-bye and cycled down the hill. Before he even got to the metro station he felt his phone ringing, and stopped short in the gutter to pull it out of his pants. The number was blocked, but he knew who it was. He let it ring several times, almost long enough to go to voice mail, and then picked up.

"Mr. Braithwaite," Frey said, skipping the pleasantries. "I understand you have some information for us."

"For you personally, actually. I don't think you'll want to be sharing this with your board."

"Can you tell me what you've found?"

"Not on the phone," Mason said. He wanted to look Frey in the eye when he told him what he knew. "Can you meet me?"

"That might be difficult today," he said. "I'm on the Westside."

"Golfing at Blue Hills?" Mason asked. "No problem—call me whenever you get a break from your investors."

"Wait," Frey said, a little too quickly. "Can you come by the office around three?"

"I'll be there," Mason said, and hung up. He started pedaling again toward the train, energized by the heady feeling of success. Mentioning Mike Valdez had worked—Frey was worried, and now he was anxious to find out what Mason knew.

Twenty minutes later he was downtown, climbing up out of the metro and locking his bike to a rack outside Miss Cassie's office building, a glamorous art deco gem from the 1930s whose interior had been converted into modern workspaces. He loved the opportunity to admire the architecture, the craftsmanship, and the murals in the lobby, despite the challenges Miss Cassie threw at him. He liked her, and she made him think about things in a constructive way sometimes, but she had some bizarre ideas about how the world worked.

He rode up in the retro mahogany-paneled elevator to her floor. The sliding sign on her door said COME IN, so he pushed it open. Miss Cassie was at her desk, on her cell phone, but she smiled and gestured to the sofa. He took his usual spot and looked out the tall windows at the towers of the financial district while he waited for her to finish. The view alone was worth coming here.

Soon she stepped around her desk and took

her chair. She was in her fifties and carried a bit of weight, and she always wore sharp suits. He wondered fleetingly how many fifty-minute hours she'd have to work in a week to cover the rent here and pay her tailor.

"So," she began, folding open her tablet and pulling out the stylus, "how is the Billy Blood psychic doing?"

"You saw that?" he asked, dismayed.

She couldn't help but smile. "I watch the news, yes. You've made quite a splash this week."

"It kind of happened without my knowledge, but I guess it's something I can use to market my services."

She started scribbling notes on her tablet. "Have you had any success with this client?"

"Yeah, and I made some money. I'm wrestling with a moral dilemma, though."

"Ah," she said, looking up from her notes and grinning. "My specialty."

"So, if I tell you something in a session, are you bound by confidentiality?"

"Of course," she said, and nodded. "Unless you tell me about committing a felony. In that case, all bets are off."

"OK," Mason said. "I'm not going to do anything like that. Basically, I have evidence that this guy, the CEO, did something shady. If it came out, it would damage his reputation and the company's too."

"If it's something true," she said, looking back to her tablet and writing, "what's the dilemma? He'll face the consequences of his actions."

"Well, if I bury it instead, nothing bad will happen. So the dilemma is whether I want to cause damage or not. I'm angry with the guy for the way he manipulated me, but I'm not sure I'm angry enough to burn down his life."

"Is what you know really all that earth-shattering?"

Mason nodded. "It is, and I have documented proof. He might even get into legal trouble."

"OK. You said there were no consequences if you don't speak out. But if he's done something dishonest, surely keeping it a secret will put somebody else at a disadvantage. Think about people who trust him in the future. You know he's not trustworthy; shouldn't you be helping them by telling them that?"

"I guess," Mason said, digesting the idea. It was a valid point, he decided.

"You also said you're angry with him," she said. "Try to visualize the situation without that. Imagine you had no strong feelings about him one way or the other. Would you speak out then?"

"Maybe. Even if I didn't know him, I could still tell that the guy's a trash bag."

"When we think about other people," Miss Cassie said, furiously scribbling notes, "it's important to separate what they do from who they are."

"I don't get what the difference is."

"People are essentially good, but they do wrong

things. He's not trash—his actions are trashy."

"Everything about him is trash," Mason said emphatically. "His actions, his attitude, his ten-thousand-dollar watch."

"Think about people who commit crimes. When someone robs a bank, they get locked up. But we don't throw away the key. If we thought the bank robber was trash, we would. People do stupid things and make mistakes, but no one is beyond redemption."

"OK," Mason said, trying to follow her rationale. "So the guy's not completely worthless. I'm sure his shareholders think he's a great man, a genius who's increasing their own net worth. But his actions are messed up."

"From your viewpoint." She looked up at him.

"Lots of other people would think so too," he said. Most definitely including Catherine.

"Back to the idea of how your actions affect people," she said. "Keeping silent has consequences just as much as speaking up does. Maybe your silence will do just as much harm to someone else."

"I'm also concerned about my own safety—I don't want it to come back on me."

"That's reasonable, but consider the impact it will have on you if you say nothing. If this man does more harm later on, how will you handle that, knowing you could have prevented it?" She looked at him over her glasses.

"You make it sound like I have no choice." He

pulled his notepad out of his backpack and made some notes of his own.

> Speaking up has consequences.
> Not speaking up does too.

"If you do decide to speak out, make sure you protect yourself first. Don't get burned when you light that match."

"Excellent advice," Mason said.

"Let's talk about decision-making in more general terms," she said, shifting in her seat. "Do you often have trouble deciding what to do?"

"No," he said, and frowned. It was an odd question, but he got into it with her, and before long their time was up.

"I hope you're able to resolve your dilemma," she said, walking him to the door.

"Thanks—I'm sure I'll sort it out."

He didn't have time to go home before meeting Frey, but he could easily work at the library, just a few blocks away. He swung by a vegan pastry shop first to fuel up on sweets, then locked up his bike outside the library and found a quiet corner where he could work.

He read through his report for Frey again, making sure he had everything straight in his mind. More than that, he was doing it to psych himself up for the confrontation. What if Frey threatened him, or worse? Frey filmed his contractors and his events as a matter of course; maybe Mason could follow his lead and film him. He pulled out his phone and spent a few minutes figuring out the video functions. He found a way to record in sixty-second chunks that would upload themselves to his online storage. A surreptitious recording wouldn't be admissible in any legal wrangling, but depending on what Frey had to say, it might be an interesting addendum to the documents Catherine had passed along.

Checking the clock, he realized it was time to go. He rode the metro to Hollywood and then cycled the last mile to the Billy Blood building. Down the block, out of sight of the front door, he locked up his bike and then pulled off his backpack, positioning his phone in the mesh pouch on the outside of the pack, intended to hold a water bottle for handy access. The elastic material kept the phone snugly in place, and he adjusted it until the camera lens had an unobstructed view through the webbing. He held the pack at arm's length to assess the overall effect; it didn't look suspicious, he decided. He hit "record" and turned off the phone's screen, repositioned it in the pouch, then walked over to the building and marched up the front steps. The door was locked, but he found an inconspicuously mounted button at one side, and pressed it. A uniformed security guard unlocked the door and stood, blocking the entrance, looking him over suspiciously.

"You're Braithwaite?" he asked.

"Yeah," Mason said.

"The CEO's in his office," he said, stepping aside

to let him in. "Third floor, left off the elevator."

No one was at the reception desk, and the building was quiet. The wall clock in the lobby said it was twenty past three—as planned, he was just late enough to imply disrespect. When the elevator doors opened, he stepped off and turned left, past the conference room where he'd first met Frey. At the end of the hall were a set of double doors, with Frey's name emblazoned on one, above the title "Chief Kid," and the other standing ajar. As he neared the door, Mason could feel his heart pounding. He knocked and stuck his head in. It was a huge room, clearly designed to awe. Full-length windows filled two walls with sweeping views of half the city, and there was enough open floor space for a soccer game. Frey was alone, sitting behind a desk that was wider than Mason's whole office.

"Mr. Braithwaite," he said, looking up from his computer. He reclined casually in his chair and laced his fingers behind his head. "Have a seat."

"Don't get up," Mason said, when he realized Frey had no intention of greeting him.

Three plush chairs were positioned in front of Frey's desk. Mason pulled off his backpack and set it on the middle one, making sure the camera lens was facing the desk, and then opened the bag to pull out the folder with the report he'd written. In his peripheral vision he saw Frey watching him, motionless. The chair might not be high enough to get Frey in the image, he realized, but there was nothing he could do about it now. Hopefully it would record more than just the blank front of his desk.

"You've been a disappointment to me," Frey said.

"You haven't even read my report yet," Mason said. Folder in hand, he dropped into one of the other chairs.

"Arko tried to set you up with several journalists this week," he said calmly, but his eyes were hard. "You kept dodging them. How difficult can it be to answer a couple of questions?"

"You should have told me up front that's what you wanted. All you asked me to do was figure out who defaced your billboard."

"About that," he said. "What have you got?"

"The answer," Mason said.

He slid the folder across the top of the desk toward Frey, who leaned forward and picked it up. He spent a few minutes reading through it, his expression impassive. Mason glanced sideways at his backpack, hoping his phone was at least picking up the audio.

"I'm surprised by this," Frey said finally, setting the folder down on his desk, his tone neutral.

Mason remembered the first insight he'd had about Frey: like digging into an onion, there were multiple layers of deception.

"Of course you are. You don't believe I'm really psychic, and you didn't really want me to find the truth—you wanted me to get media attention for your product."

"None of this is true. It's a series of wild and

spurious accusations with no merit."

"Man, don't even go there," Mason said. "You can't bullshit me anymore. I can pull information out of inanimate objects, and travel through time. Do you really think I can't see through this two-bit subterfuge?"

Frey stared at him for a minute, calculating. "You remember that you signed a nondisclosure agreement, don't you? If any of this came out, I'd have to sue you. You know I have considerable resources for that kind of undertaking. I'd bury you."

Mason laughed. "I'm no lawyer, but my understanding is that contracts can't be binding if they involve breaking the law. Do you think Valdez over at Mangel and Stein would back up what you've said to the media? Five minutes into a deposition, he'd sing like a bird."

It was bluster on Mason's part, but he could see in Frey's expression that he believed it. If he couldn't trust his coconspirators, he'd never launch a lawsuit.

"You've spoken to Valdez?" Frey asked. "That surprises me too."

"It doesn't matter who I talked to. What's in the folder is the truth." He wondered fleetingly if he had put Valdez in danger by letting Frey assume he had talked to Mason. But Valdez worked for canny lawyers, and could take care of himself. Mason had his own concerns right now.

Frey sighed and rubbed his eyes, sinking back in his chair. For the first time, he looked like an ordinary person, no longer puffed up and authoritative.

"So, why me?" Mason asked.

"What are you talking about?"

"Why did you play me? You could have hired an actor to play a psychic and get all the media coverage you want."

"It wouldn't have looked real if I'd hired an actor. Any decent journalist would have smelled that right away. You're an actual psychic, but my mistake was in thinking you'd already have media experience, that you'd be comfortable with filming." His lip curled in disgust. "What kind of LA psychic doesn't know how to work with a camera?"

"Me," Mason said simply. He doubted any of Hanh's posse had spent time producing media content either, but Frey lived in a different version of LA.

"Like I said, a disappointment. I also thought it would be less suspicious if it looked like I was taking measures to find the culprit. You were much less likely to figure it out than the police."

Mason nodded. Finally, the truth.

"Plus, people love freaks—and you walked right into my lap." He grinned at the memory. "How could I say no to a psychic circus? I just wish you'd been better at it."

Mason bristled. "Things would have gone differently if you'd explained you wanted a circus—I wouldn't have signed on. But I can whip up a circus now that I know the whole story. Maybe I should talk to some of the journalists you've been throwing at me."

"You'll keep your damn mouth shut." Frey sat forward, his eyes smoldering and locked on Mason's. "I might not be able to sue you, but I'm not above a little old-fashioned violence. You don't know who I am."

Mason wanted to say, "You're a thug," but he knew Frey wasn't bluffing—anyone protecting a billion-dollar enterprise would be capable of terrible things. The thought of it made his skin crawl, but he refused to be intimidated.

"How about this," Mason said. "Pay me what you owe me, and we're done."

"I'm not going to be extorted."

"I don't want your fucking money," Mason snapped, insulted at being taken for a thief. "I want you to pay me the rest of what we agreed to—twenty-five hundred, nothing more. I'm not going to blackmail you."

"That makes no sense," Frey said.

"Not to you, because you have no morals."

Frey's face contorted with anger. "Be warned," he said tersely. "If you make me look bad, I am going to come after you, and I am going to fuck you up."

"Bring it on," Mason said, raising his voice and jutting out his chin. It was swagger, and he really was afraid of this man right now, but at least things weren't going to get violent this second. He stood up and pulled on his backpack, and walked toward the door.

"I'm not kidding," Frey called after him.

"Pay me," Mason said, not looking back.

He smiled to himself as he boarded the elevator. That last part, yelling at Mason as he left, was an act of desperation more than anger. It meant that Frey was running scared and felt he was losing control, despite his threats. And if he was scared of Mason, Mason still had power over him.

He waited until he was partway down the block, then looked over his shoulder to make sure he wasn't being observed before he pulled his phone out of his backpack and switched off the camera. He'd check out the video later. Right now he just wanted to get away from here. He could still feel the adrenaline pounding in his veins as he unlocked his bike, and he pedaled hard to burn it off. If he had to make the call right now, he'd definitely expose Frey. He wasn't afraid of getting sued anymore, because Frey knew it wasn't a viable option. He wasn't sure how seriously he should take the threat of violence, although he believed Frey was capable of it. But he wasn't going to let that make up his mind. Even with Miss Cassie's spin on things, he still couldn't see a clear path ahead. Maybe there was a way for the truth to come out without implicating Mason.

At home he had a long shower and then examined the video he'd taken. He was happy to find the entire encounter had been recorded successfully, and took a few minutes to splice all the minute-long chunks together into one file. He set it aside and spent some time reading email and news. Eventually Ned started puttering in the kitchen, and Mason went out to join him, sitting across the counter on one of the barstools.

"How was Miss Cassie?" Ned asked. He was slicing onions into tiny ribbons.

"It was OK. We talked about whether I should release Catherine's evidence."

"What did you decide?"

"I haven't yet. I also went to see Frey at Billy Blood. I taped our meeting. Want to see it?"

Ned's eyes grew wide. "He let you do that?"

"He had no idea."

A smile spread across Ned's face. "You devious little monkey. You do know that you can't record people without their permission, right?"

"It's not like I'm going to put it online or send it to his investors. I knew he'd be upset that I figured out what he was up to, and I wanted to have a record of that." He drummed his fingers on the countertop. "So do you want to see it?"

"Hell, yes," Ned said, setting down his knife and wiping his hands on his apron.

Mason went to the office and came back with his laptop, setting it on the bar and positioning it so they could both see the screen. He pulled up the video, queued it to where he'd sat down with Frey, and pressed "play."

"You've been a disappointment to me," Frey said, his voice small and tinny through the little speakers. The lower third of the video frame was the wood-grain front of his desk, but the top part had caught Frey from the chest up.

Ned was transfixed, and reacted physically when Frey threatened Mason, involuntarily pulling back from the screen. Mason stopped the video after he'd picked up his bag and walked out of Frey's office.

"You can really be tough when you need to be," Ned said, looking dazed. "You handled him well. But he actually threatened you with violence. Doesn't that make you want to back off?"

"I guess I'm trying to stay rational. I'm sure he's capable of violence, but I'm not too worried about it. It's like when those preschoolers yell 'Stay out of our day care' when you walk past their fence. It's not a legitimate threat."

"Frey runs a billion-dollar corporation. He's not a preschooler," Ned said. "He could make you disappear without a trace."

"He won't, though. If I don't say anything, he won't have any reason to come after me. And if I do, he'll be so busy with damage control that he won't have time to worry about me."

Ned thought for a moment. "That actually sounds right. I just don't want you to get hurt."

Mason could see the concern in his eyes. "I won't," he said. "But it still comes down to whether or not I want to take down Tyler Frey."

"*Chupacabra,*" Ned said. He picked up his knife and went back to the onions. "Think about the goats. If you speak up, you could slow down the demand for Billy Blood, and save a few lives."

"I hadn't even thought of that," Mason said. It was another good reason to speak out.

Before long Ned had cooked the onions and some tomatoes and rice into a delectable paella. They ate on the balcony in the fading daylight. Afterward, Mason wanted to decompress from the excitement of the day, so he watched an episode of *Pica Confessions* with Ned. Seeing the protagonist eating drywall got him thinking about Matt, the biologist they'd rescued in Hanh's back room, and what he'd said about Billy Blood. He'd talked about prions. Mason looked for articles online, and spent the rest of the evening reading about how prions work and how they can affect people.

Eventually he climbed into bed, soon followed by Ned, who straddled him and grabbed his hands.

"What's this?" Mason asked, laughing at his playfulness.

"Where's the hard-ass Mason from the video?" he asked. "'I don't want your fucking money,'" he barked.

"He's around," Mason said, pulling his hands free and sliding them into Ned's hair. "Maybe you want him to fuck you up."

"Bring it on," Ned said.

Before he drifted into sleep he told himself to dream about how to handle Catherine's documents. He needed some inspiration. "You'll know what to do in the morning," he told himself.

He slept soundly, after such a long day, and didn't dream of anything particularly significant, but he definitely figured out what to do.

Sunday

The morning brought newfound resolve. By the time Mason rolled out of bed, Ned had already gone to see his parents, and Peggy was spending the day with her brother, so he had the house to himself. After a couple of pots of espresso and some fruit, he took his laptop out on the balcony, shivering at first in the cool air.

Danny Santos, it turned out, was a serious journalist. He'd done investigative work on sleaze in local governments, unions, and school boards. Mason read several of his pieces to find out if Santos used anonymous sources; he often did, it turned out. He wondered if there had ever been any fallout from that, but couldn't find anything that suggested

Santos had ever burned a source, or been challenged on it. It seemed like he had integrity, despite the connection to Gilbert.

He pulled his phone out of his pocket and dialed Gilbert's number.

"Nelson Wrathway," Gilbert answered. "How's it going?"

"How do you know Danny Santos?" Mason asked, getting right to the point.

"We grew up on the same block," Gilbert said. "Ned might remember him too—we all went to middle school together."

"I want you to do me a favor," Mason said. "Set up a meeting with him for me. Somewhere private, like your place. I don't want him coming over here."

"Sure, buddy. Is it about Billy Blood?"

"Yeah—but you can't tell anyone else."

"It sounds serious."

"It is. If they find out I've been talking to a reporter, they'll hunt me down and break my knee-caps—or worse."

"Damn," Gilbert said, pausing to absorb it all. "I'll talk to him today," he said finally, his voice just above a whisper. "I'll leave your name out of it until I get a meeting set up."

"Thanks, man. I owe you one."

A call had come in while he'd been on the phone with Gilbert. He didn't recognize the number, but the caller had left a voice mail.

"Hey man," the recording began. "It's Matt, from

Hanh's salon the other night. Can we talk?"

So many people were entangled with Billy Blood and its bloody sugar water. Mason called him back.

"Yo," Matt said when he picked up.

"It sounds like you're in better shape than you were the other night," Mason said.

"Almost back to normal," Matt said. "I wanted to talk about the goat suckers."

"I'm around today," Mason said. "What part of town are you in?"

"I live in the Arts District."

"OK—do you know that vegan diner on Second Street, near the metro?"

"I love that place," Matt said. "I'm vegan too. And with what I've been learning, it's a good time to be."

They made a plan to meet later in the day. After he hung up, Mason thought about him for a minute. They had a lot in common, from the inept temporal bleed-throughs to digging up dirt on Billy Blood; maybe they could pool their resources. But he had a lot to do today first.

He opened Catherine's document, pausing for a second to remember the password he'd put on it, and looked through the pages. It was so incriminating, he felt nervous just being in possession of it. He glanced over his shoulder into the house, even though he knew no one was there to see what he was reading.

He was going to give this to Santos, but not as a computer file. It would almost certainly have a digital trail leading directly to Mason embedded in it, having been on his laptop, and every copy made would perfectly reproduce that. The advantage of paper was that any identifying information, like his actual fingerprints, would be lost with each copy made. He didn't want to print it on Ned's office printer, though. Gilbert had once told them that every printer was programmed to put imperceptible identifying information, like a serial number, on every page, so that law enforcement could trace any sheet of paper back to the printer's owner. At the time Mason had dismissed it as far-fetched, but it was easy enough to print this out anonymously—and he knew exactly where to go to distance himself from the possibility of being identified later.

He folded his laptop closed and went inside to stuff it into his backpack. A few minutes later he was cycling along a commercial strip not far from their neighborhood, where there was a tiny street-front packing-and-shipping store. There were no security cameras at the entrance, but he parked his bike down the block anyway, then walked up to it.

The door chimed when he stepped into the cramped interior, fluorescent-lit and devoid of life. He'd been in here a year or two ago, and the place hadn't changed at all. There were stacks of flat moving boxes and rolls of bubble wrap and packing tape; in a corner stood a photocopier. A cursory glance at the ceiling revealed no cameras inside either. As he'd expected, this place was old-school about security—

which made sense since there wasn't anything worth stealing.

A woman came to the counter from the back room, her blue-gray hair sensibly shorn. The way she claimed the space told Mason she was the proprietor rather than a staffer.

"Can I help you?" she asked.

"I want to print about forty pages from my computer," he said. "Can you do that?"

"Sure."

Mason pulled out his laptop and set it on the counter, and she explained how to connect to her network. Mason found the printer and sent Catherine's document to it, pulling the sheets from the machine after they'd printed and stuffing them into his backpack, then closing his laptop and putting it away too.

"How much?" he asked, and pulled a wad of cash from his pants pocket.

"Seven eighty-five." After she had made change, she said, "Can I ask your name? Just for my records." Her fingers hovered over her keyboard expectantly.

"Yeah—it's Tyler Frey. F-R-E-Y."

"Great," she said, clacking at her keyboard. She looked up and smiled. "Do you live in the neighborhood, Tyler?"

"No, I'm just passing through. But I'm glad I saw your shop." He nodded and stepped out into the street.

That was creepy, he thought as he walked to his

bike. But was it really? She was likely just an amiable shopkeeper trying to build her customer base, but the newly paranoid circuits in his brain insisted there was more to it. In that case, lying about his name was pointless: connecting his computer to the shop's network would have told her exactly who he was, and the photocopier could have sent copies of his prints to some other nefarious database, all of which negated any anonymity gained by using someone else's printer.

Stop it, he admonished himself. Stop seeing the world through Gilbert's eyes. It was hard enough integrating his own shifting understanding of reality, his expanding psychic skills, without taking on conspiracies about control and manipulation by hidden forces. If he kept this up, he'd wind up completely paralyzed, wearing a foil hat and cowering from the aliens on the roof.

He put it out of his mind and unlocked his bike, cycling toward the metro. With a change of trains he was soon carrying his bicycle off the platform in the Arts District, a dense little neighborhood in the east part of downtown. It had once been mostly light industrial warehouses where bona fide working artists had pioneered studio spaces, but like so many central neighborhoods, now it was all about luxury condos, chain stores, and fancy cafés. Artists certainly couldn't afford to live around here anymore.

He scanned the lunch crowd at the tables along the sidewalk as he locked up his bike across the street from the diner. Matt spotted him and waved him over. Mason hardly recognized him: he had shaved off his thick beard and trimmed his hair, now neatly tied at the back of his head. He was dressed casually in shorts and a T-shirt.

"You look like a twenty-first-century guy," Mason said as he sat down across from him. "And you smell like one too."

Matt laughed. "I was gone so long I guess I forgot what being clean was like."

Mason caught the waitress's eye and mouthed "coffee"; Matt already had one. "Why did you go so far? That's kind of unusual, isn't it?"

Matt looked a little sheepish. "I'd never done it before. I guess I got carried away. I should have tried to come back sooner, but I got caught up in it. I started to forget where I was from."

"How did Hanh know you needed help to get back?"

"No clue. I'd never seen her before. She was really good to me, though. Without her I'd be fucked. I wish I knew how she found me."

"Me too," Mason said. He was glad he wasn't the only one who found her enigmatic, and it made him want to ask her to explain what had happened at the séance. "You went to research plants, right?"

"Liverworts. It's my field. I wanted to find out which species grew here originally. There's no way to find that out today—everything's either paved over or contaminated with nonnative species."

The waitress set a mug in front of Mason and

asked, "Something to eat, boys?"

"I want the tempeh reuben," Matt said. "And go heavy on the slaw."

"Oh, yeah, that sounds good," Mason said. "The same for me."

"You've done it too, haven't you?" Matt asked him when she'd gone.

"The bleed-through? I have. I needed help getting back the first time I did it too, even though I was only gone for a day. Since then I've mostly just done the visual bleed-through, where you can see things but you're not really there."

Matt nodded and sipped his coffee. "Have you always had psychic experiences?"

"I think so, but I kind of tuned them out until recently. I remember things happening way back in childhood."

"Did you hit your head one day or something?"

Mason laughed. "No—I think it was always just part of me."

"Me too," Matt said. "There was no initiating event. I remember sitting in the kitchen when I was a toddler, and someone stepped into the room out of nowhere. Someone without a body, like a projection. She looked like a cloud of smoke. I was so young that I didn't think it was weird, and I just watched her. She was looking around, and then she realized that I could see her, and poof—she was gone."

"Cool," Mason said. "It sounds like you were tuned in early on."

"I think I was just more observant than most kids. I had a lot more time to think because I was always off on my own, reading a book or playing with frogs."

"That's where I first saw you—in the mud, messing around at the riverbank." Mason sipped from his cup, and then said, "So why would a psychic kid become a scientist?"

"Critters," Matt said. "I was enraptured with them. That's why I'm vegan too. I don't think science is in any way incompatible with the psychic stuff, by the way—scientists just need to open their minds a little more."

"Right on," Mason said. He wanted Ned to talk to this guy.

The waitress brought their food, and Mason dug in.

After he'd taken a few bites, Matt set his sandwich down and said, "I wanted to talk about the Billy Blood thing. You said you knew the CEO, Tyler Frey. Is there any way you could arrange a sit-down with him?"

"Frey is done with me," Mason said. "We didn't part on good terms." He explained how Frey had manipulated him in the hope of getting media coverage, but didn't get into the confrontation they'd had yesterday.

"What a dick," Matt said. "I'm sure he won't even give me the time of day without an intro. That's disappointing—I want to tell someone in management about the prion thing. I talked to the guy in China who formulated that shit, but he's just a subcontractor. He completely dismissed me as a crank."

"How did you manage to find him?" Mason asked.

"I found a grad student who speaks Mandarin, and we figured out who was brewing it." He sighed. "I'm not even completely sure the prions are really in there. It depends on how it's processed, right, and that's all done in China, so who the fuck knows?"

"I read up on prions, but I couldn't find anything about plant prions being dangerous."

"I'm thinking now that it's not from the liverwort. The Chinese plant contains the prion, but the same species I collected on my little excursion tested negative for it. I didn't get much time to verify that, because Hanh confiscated my samples."

"Why would she do that?"

"I have no idea. She drove over to campus and came into my lab, made me hand them over, like she was a goddamn cop." He smiled faintly and shook his head, more bemused than upset.

"Ouch," Mason said.

"But my new theory is that it's something about how the plants are grown. In China everything is fertilized with industrial animal manure, which is completely stupid—if the animals have the prion, the plants can pick it up from the soil—and then you're consuming a mammalian prion in your salad."

"That's terrifying."

"I know. It also means some batches of Billy

Blood might contain the prion, and others won't. It depends on what the ingredients were grown in." He pushed his plate away. "So you grind up dead sheep, feed them to cattle, then fertilize your herb garden with cow shit and carcasses. What could possibly go wrong?"

"If you can't get the company to listen to you, what's the next step?" Mason asked.

"I know a woman from when I was in grad school who works for the FDA now. Maybe she'll have some ideas."

"It would be great to get the feds to shut it down," Mason said, picking up his coffee mug. "Or at least look into it."

"It'd be quicker to get the company to change the formula. Bureaucracy moves at a glacial pace. But it's probably good that you're done with Billy Blood. If this prion thing blows up—and I'm hoping it will—it might get ugly."

"You know, I've got my own Billy Blood thing going on—I've got evidence of Frey basically committing fraud, and I'm going to publicize it."

"Will it put him out of business?" Matt asked hopefully.

"I doubt that, but at a minimum it'll give the company a black eye." He thought for a minute. "I wonder if we can coordinate the timing? If the prion thing came out first, my dirt on Frey would hit them like a second blow, maybe make them scramble harder."

"Sure, but I have no idea when, or if, I can get

the feds to do anything. Is your thing something you can sit on?"

"No, it's not. I'm going to talk to a newspaper guy about it soon, and after that it'll be on his timetable."

"Well, I hope one of us gets some attention," Matt said, leaning back in his chair.

Mason brought the conversation back to psychic matters, asking Matt about some of his techniques, and shared his own ideas about lucid dreaming and psychometry. By the time they'd split the bill and parted ways, Mason felt he had a new peer. Laura would approve, at least; on that front he was doing exactly what she'd suggested—connecting with others in the field.

Before he pedaled away, he checked his phone, and found a text from Gilbert: "Drop by after nine. My friend will be here."

"I want to talk to you first," he wrote back. "Can I come at eight thirty?"

"Come whenever," Gilbert texted. "I'm here."

Rather than heading home, Mason took the metro to Hollywood and cycled to Hanh's shop. He considered phoning her first, but he knew she'd probably be there, and catching someone off guard was useful in making them more forthcoming.

The woman at the reception desk recognized Mason when he stepped inside.

"You want to see Miss Hanh?" she asked, summoning her by telephone when Mason nodded.

The shop had just a couple of weekend staff tending to customers at the nail stations, and soon Hanh appeared from the back room.

"Let me see," she said, gesturing for his hands. She examined his nails for a moment. "Your manicure is still flawless. Did you perhaps have another reason for dropping by?" she asked, arching her eyebrows.

"I was hoping you'd have a minute to chat."

She grinned and said, "Let's have a coffee. Come on back."

He followed her into the storeroom, where the round table was still set up with the chairs around it. Hanh pulled the half-empty carafe from an ancient, grubby coffeemaker that was nestled on the supply shelves amid the bottles of chemicals and towels, and poured the contents into two mugs, handing one to Mason. He wasn't a fan of the coffee produced by such devices, but he wasn't going to turn down caffeine. She gestured for him to sit, and they both took the places they'd occupied at the séance.

"You're looking for answers," she said.

"Yes. How did we do what we did?"

She smiled and watched him for a few seconds before speaking. "The rational mind just won't let go. Everything must be explained."

"It's hard not to think that way."

She looked down and furrowed her brow, remembering. "To pull Matt back, we needed all five psychics. Our combined energy formed a gestalt. One of us alone wouldn't have been able to do that."

"I figured as much," Mason said. "How did you know he needed help in the first place?"

She took a swig of coffee and met his eye. "I've taken on responsibility for some of you. It's kind of a volunteer project."

"Meaning those of us who aren't great at it yet?"

"Psychics who haven't had a lot of practice, or people who bleed through unintentionally. I keep my third eye peeled for trouble, and sometimes Laura passes me information. When you bled through, I was able to go myself, but Matt went too far. It was safer to do it remotely."

"How do you know that, though?" Mason asked. He wrapped both hands around his mug. "What exactly is your third eye?"

"It's what we all do, as psychics, just more finely tuned to specific criteria. The information is there for anyone to see, but I'm able to bring it into focus. Think of all the radio waves bouncing around. All kinds of phone and Wi-Fi and TV signals surround us all the time, but we're oblivious to their existence. With the right equipment, though, it's possible to decode them. Like a psychic police scanner."

"OK, that makes sense," he said. "What about the mechanism of bleeding through? How does that work?"

"Have you heard the idea that eternity is all around us?" she asked.

"Sure. It comes up a lot in books about paranormal phenomena."

"What does it mean to you?"

"Well, in psychic terms, I think everything's connected. I can access information that might seem lost, or hidden, or too far away."

"Right. Time works that way too—every moment is connected. Every moment exists all around us, right now. Bleeding through to the 1790s is possible because the 1790s are happening right now."

Mason nodded. It made sense instinctively, the way the idea felt in his mind. If he tried to parse it rationally, though, it started to escape him.

"We can talk about it all day and not accomplish anything," she said, and stood, picking up the mugs. "I encourage you just to do it, and stop worrying about how you're doing it. It's like riding your bicycle: once it's in your muscle memory, you don't even have to think about it."

It was sage advice, he suspected. "Thanks for the coffee, and the answers," he said with a grin, rising from the table.

He tried to digest what she'd said on the ride home. It was still woolly and vague, but he knew it wasn't going to get any clearer. He needed to take her advice and just let it happen—embrace his psychic experiences as achievable but inherently inexplicable.

Peggy was home when he got in, banging around in her room. Mason stuck his head in to say hello. There were clothes everywhere. She was standing in front of her closet, and appeared to be cleaning it out.

"How's Andy?" he asked, taking in the mess. He knew Peggy had spent the day with her half-brother. She'd only recently met him, with Mason's help, and they were developing a bond.

"He's great," she said. "We worked on some music, and had lunch near his place. I never go over there, so it was fun to explore the neighborhood."

"Cleaning day?"

"Yeah, time to make some room and donate the surplus." She held a baggy floral-print blouse up to her chest. "Is this too old?"

"You're asking me? I buy all my clothes at thrift stores. Someone told me the other day my new shirt had been on the runway two years ago."

"I meant is it too old for me. Does it make me look like a granny?"

"I can't help you, sister," he said, spreading his palms. "All I see is fabric and flowers."

"I'll ask Ned," she said, and threw it on the pile on her bed.

"He texted that he's staying for dinner with his family."

"You're not going over?"

"I have a meeting later, so I'm going to eat here." He watched her for a minute, flicking through her hanging clothes, pulling out every fifth or sixth garment to throw on one of the piles. "I wonder if there's anything to eat," he said finally.

"If you can wait half an hour, I'll make us dinner," she said.

"What a great idea."

Before long Mason heard her in the kitchen. He went out and asked, "Can I help?"

"You can tell me about your day," she said. "I'm going to make tabbouleh with quinoa instead of wheat, how does that sound?"

"Amazing," he said, and climbed onto a barstool. "So I hung out today with Matt, that guy we brought back in the séance. He's in a similar place, still learning the psychic techniques."

"Is he someone who might become a friend?" She had piled three massive bunches of parsley on the cutting board, and started chopping it into tiny bits.

"Maybe," Mason said. "But I may not be LA's premier vegan psychic anymore."

She laughed. "Is he a competitor?"

"No—he's a biologist, at Cal State LA. He just uses the psychic stuff for his own purposes."

"Then you're still LA's premier vegan psychic investigator. Is he straight?"

"I think so," he said. "My gaydar says eighty percent probability."

"What does he look like?"

"Ordinary. Not bad looking. Five-foot-ten, lots of hair. And scrawny, after living in the eighteenth century for six weeks."

She laughed. "Maybe you can introduce us, then. I've been single long enough."

They ate the tabbouleh with some pita bread and leftover cucumber salad on the side, and Mason cleaned up the kitchen. He was nervous about meeting Santos, but he knew it was the right thing to do. Resolute, he pulled on his backpack, checking that Catherine's printouts were still there, and went out to his bike. Gilbert's place wasn't far away, but Mason wasn't willing to ride over there in the dark—not yet—so he waited for the bus, and loaded his bike on the front rack.

The streets were quieter from the main road to Gilbert's, but the hills were steep, and he was winded when he got there. Gilbert's apartment was the entire second floor, but he saw that the windows were dark. No one had lived in the first-floor apartment for years, since the building had been yellow-tagged in an earthquake, and legally Gilbert wasn't supposed to be living there either, but he had a knack for flying under the radar. But why was it so dark?

He started up the driveway, but stopped before he reached the foot of the stairs up to Gilbert's door. It was inky black, beyond the range of the sparse streetlights. He waited a minute for his eyes to adjust. He could make out the eaves far above, and thought about the aliens Gilbert said he'd heard moving around up there at night. A flash of fear ran through him at the thought of one of them peering down over the rain gutter at him. He looked away and said aloud, "I reject Gilbert's worldview."

It was too dark to see up the stairs, so he pulled out his phone and turned the flashlight function on. In the dream he'd had about hunting for Frey in the dark, he remembered, he had held the torch up above his head. Holding his phone up high like that worked—he could see the way now. He climbed the stairs, the circle of light ascending before him, illuminating the darkness ahead.

There was no bell, so he knocked on the door. His knuckles made almost no sound, as the door was heavy and lined with steel, so he pounded on it with his fist. He wasn't even sure Gilbert was here, with all the lights out.

But he was: Gilbert pulled open the door and welcomed him in. The room was lit normally, with ceiling lights reflecting on the hardwood floor, and a lamp illuminating his messy desk, piled high with books and paper.

"Those must be heavy drapes," Mason said. "I thought you weren't home."

"Check it out," Gilbert said, and pulled aside the curtain next to his desk. The window was completely papered over with aluminum foil.

"Why would you do that?" Mason asked, dumbfounded.

"It cuts down on radio frequencies," he said. "Plus, no one can see in."

"Is every window like that? Even your bedroom?" Gilbert nodded.

"Don't you miss the sunshine?" Mason asked. He

couldn't believe anyone would choose to live without daylight.

"We go up on the roof for breakfast, and to read sometimes. It's nice up there, and I get all the vitamin D I need. I just have to make sure none of the darknet satellites are out when I'm up there. But they're only overhead a few minutes a day, and people post the schedules online, so it's easy to avoid them."

Mason looked at him, at a loss. Was he seriously concerned about being photographed by satellites?

Misinterpreting Mason's silence as concern, Gilbert said, "Don't worry—I'm safer this way." He strode over to the kitchenette and pulled open the fridge. "Do you want a beer?"

"No, man, I want to keep a clear head."

"OK—me too, then." He closed the fridge and waved at the sofa. "Sit down."

Mason moved some magazines and a sweatshirt from one end of the sagging plaid monstrosity, then sat down carefully.

Gilbert sat in his equally well-worn recliner and tented his fingers. "You said you wanted to talk to me before Danny got here," he said, looking at Mason expectantly.

"I'd like to show you what I'm going to give him. But you have to promise you won't say anything about it to anyone."

"Sure," he said. "You have dirt on Billy Blood, and you don't want them to know you're the source."

"It's more than that—Gilbert, you were right

about everything." He sat forward and spoke ear-nestly. "That woman *is* NSA, and she was in town to investigate Frey and Billy Blood. She passed me this stuff...." He pulled the sheaf of paper out of his backpack and held it up, but didn't give it to him yet. "It proves that Frey arranged for his own vandalism, and I want Danny to write about that. But he can't know it came from the NSA. You have to keep my secret. You know what can happen if you cross those people."

Gilbert's eyes had grown wide. He nodded slowly.

"I'm trusting you, man. Don't let me down," Mason said, and gingerly handed the papers over to him.

Gilbert took the pages and quickly started read-ing, occasionally clicking his tongue in disbelief. It was a gamble to take Gilbert completely into his confidence, Mason knew, but it was also risky to share something with Santos and not with Gilbert— Gilbert might have pestered both of them until he found out or, worse, asked someone else about it, like his online conspiracy cohorts. He felt bad about playing to Gilbert's fears of the government's secre-tive machinations, but speaking Gilbert's language was the best way to get him on board.

"This is totally NSA stuff," Gilbert said excitedly, looking up after reading the last page. "The phone transcripts are all in caps—they do that because their transcription machines are old, like 1980s-era, when computers only knew how to do caps."

"Danny doesn't need to know that, though. I'm not going to tell him. It's the only way I'll be safe."

"I get it," Gilbert said, passing the paperwork back to Mason. He sat back it the chair, a faraway look in his eyes.

"Are you OK?" Mason asked him.

"Yeah—it's just not very often that I get confirmation. I knew she was NSA, and then you got the proof." He sat quietly for a minute. "It makes me wonder if I can get proof about the aliens."

"Let's not worry about that tonight," Mason said quickly. "Let me deal with Danny first."

Santos soon arrived, announcing himself with a dull thumping on the door. Gilbert got up to let him in, and Mason rose to greet him. He had dark hair, like Gilbert, and wore jeans and a vest over his shirt.

"The Billy Blood psychic," Santos said. "I called you the other day, and you blew me off."

"I didn't think I had anything newsworthy then," Mason said, "but I do now. I'm Mason."

Santos nodded and turned to Gilbert. "Why all the secrecy? You could have told me who you wanted me to meet."

"They'll break his kneecaps if they find out he talked to you," Gilbert said. "I was trying to keep Mason safe."

Santos looked at Mason with a wry smile. "I'm looking forward to this."

"Sit down," Gilbert said.

"Do you have a kitchen table or something?"

Santos said, looking askance at the dilapidated sofa.

"It's on the roof," Gilbert said. "It's too dark to sit up there now." He stepped around to the other end of the sofa and cleared a space for himself to sit. "Take the chair," he told Santos.

Once he'd settled into the recliner, Santos said, "I was approaching the Billy Blood thing as an entertainment story, because that seemed to be the only value in it. What could you possibly have on them that would make them want to harm you?"

"First off," Mason said, "can I speak as an anonymous source?"

"Sure. I can't guarantee I'll use what you've got, but I can keep your name out of it."

Mason took a deep breath. "It's all in here. You can keep these copies." He handed the sheaf of paper over.

Santos looked him in the eye as he took the paperwork, then pulled a pair of reading glasses out of his shirt pocket and read intently, flipping through the pages one by one.

They sat in silence to let him read. The house was quiet, except for the sofa complaining now and then when Gilbert fidgeted. No sign of aliens on the roof yet, Mason thought.

"Where did this come from?" Santos said finally, pulling off his glasses and looking up at Mason.

"I can't tell you."

"I know it isn't from Billy Blood, because some of it is internal stuff from the lawyers. Billy Blood wouldn't have access to that."

He was sharp, Mason realized.

Santos riffled through the pages. "Surely you didn't run your own wiretap on Mangel and Stein?"

"I don't have those kinds of resources," Mason said.

"OK." He watched Mason for a few seconds. "You understand that I can't use this without some corroboration, right? It could all be made up."

"He didn't make it up," Gilbert said sharply.

Mason laughed, and said, "Thanks, Gilbert—but he does have a point." And to Santos, "I'm pretty sure the only person at Billy Blood who knows about this is Frey himself. I bounced it off Arko Ramsey, their PR guy, but he's clueless. Your best bet might be to locate Hector, the guy who did the actual paint job— his name's in there, and his phone number."

"That might work," Santos said, "if I could get him to admit to it."

"In the phone transcripts, Mike Valdez was kind of mean to him, and dismissive. You might be able to exploit that—make him feel like you understand that Valdez bullied him."

"Good," Santos said emphatically, and groped at his pants pockets until he found a pen. He fumbled with his glasses to get them back on his face, then flipped to the relevant sheet and started writing notes in the margin, cradling the pages in his lap.

"Mike Valdez was Frey's contact at the law firm, and when I confronted Frey about all this, he implied that he didn't trust Valdez to keep quiet. He works for lawyers, so he probably won't talk to you, but he's another person who could confirm the story."

Santos asked a few more questions, trying to elicit further details, and Mason answered what he could without talking about Catherine. Santos spent a few more minutes making notes, then sat back in the chair. "I like this. If I can get one of these guys to confirm enough of it, I'll write it up. It's going to be tricky if none of the principals will talk, but I'll try."

"I understand," Mason said.

Santos rose and folded the sheaf of paper in half. "I'll be in touch," he said, and Gilbert followed him to the door.

"Don't forget, Mason's name has to stay out of it," Gilbert reminded him.

"I think I'll remember that," he said with a grin, and bade them good-night.

"You did it, man," Gilbert said, closing the door after Santos had left. "You're sticking it to the man."

"I hope so," Mason said. "I guess we'll see what happens." He could already feel his anxiety about Catherine's documents evaporating—he'd made his play. "How about that beer?"

Gilbert brought them each a bottle, and they sat for a while, chatting about Santos, and then about Harmony, and Peggy, and Ned.

"I should go," Mason said, after he'd finished the bottle. "I'm glad the aliens didn't visit tonight."

Gilbert's face clouded. "They wait till I'm asleep."

Mason stood and pulled on his backpack. "Did you ever try telling them to leave?"

"Seriously? Is that psychic advice?"

"Kind of. Say it in your mind, in case they can pick that up, and say it out loud. It's worth a try."

"Sure," Gilbert said, and smiled wanly, then gave Mason a hug before he left.

Ned was home when he got in, sprawled on the sofa with his tablet. "My mom sent you some rice," he said.

"I love that woman," Mason said. He left his backpack by the door and found the container in the fridge, then took a fork and sat on the sofa at Ned's feet.

"Do you remember a guy named Danny Santos?" he asked.

"Sure. He was more Gilbert's friend than mine, but I know him. He writes for *Va-Voom*."

"I know," Mason said, and between mouthfuls he told him about his evening.

"I'm glad you decided to do that," Ned said, moving his bare feet into Mason's lap.

"I just hope he can make it happen," Mason said.

"At least you don't have to worry about it anymore—it's out of your hands."

Later, when they went to bed, Mason rapidly drifted into the hypnagogic state, and reminded himself to wake up inside his dreams. At some point he became aware that he was floating, on his back, in pleasantly warm water. A swimming pool, he realized, seeing its edges in his peripheral vision. But more interesting was the sky above, in a wide gamut of blue, lighter at the horizon and indigo above. It was that delightful time of day when the stars were becoming visible—bright ones at first, and others gradually winking into view. He watched the show, appreciating the warmth, and the quiet, and the calm.

Monday

Aweek later, Mason had mostly managed to put the Billy Blood case behind him. He hadn't heard from Frey again, but a check had come on Thursday for the balance of Mason's fee. Arko had attached a handwritten sticky note that said, "Hope to see you again soon," consummated with a smiley face. It wasn't likely they'd be working together again, but he was a nice enough guy, and Mason couldn't write him off just because he worked for a lowlife.

He was starting to think it was time to look for some new clients, but he had enjoyed the week off since he talked to Danny Santos, and a few more days wouldn't hurt. He'd also begun to wonder whether

Santos had had any luck pursuing the story. He didn't want to bug the guy, but he'd considered checking in with Gilbert. He watched for news reports about Billy Blood, and checked at least once a day to make sure there were no new stories with Mason or Nelson Wrathway in them.

He didn't have to call Gilbert, though, because Gilbert called him. Mason was sitting on the balcony, his computer open on his lap, enjoying the warm afternoon.

"I have a hot tip," he said when Mason answered. "Danny's done it—the story went live this morning."

"Seriously?" Mason said, sitting up in his chair. "It's on the *Va-Voom* website?"

"Yeah, but Danny says it's going to be all over the place. He figures it's big enough that it'll even be on national TV. It's on channel six right now."

It was the station that had done the original report on Billy Blood's psychic research, and it was where Frey had worked—it would be especially embarrassing for Frey if his old friends were covering Santos's story.

Ned was in the office, and Mason leaned into the open French doors and shouted for him.

"What's with the hollering?" Ned asked when he came out.

"Danny Santos's story came out today. Do you want to watch?"

"Of course," he said, and dropped into a chair on the balcony. Mason twisted his laptop so they could both see, and pulled up the station's website to watch the piece from the beginning.

"Explosive allegations about the lifestyle drink Billy Blood have surfaced from several sources," the newsreader began, the familiar acid-yellow logo floating over his right shoulder. "Federal authorities announced earlier today that they're investigating reports that Billy Blood contains prions," pronouncing the word as if it had never been spoken before, "a toxic ingredient that can be dangerous"—he paused for effect—"to human health."

Mason paused the video. "That's Matt's story, not Santos's," he said. "His FDA contact must have come through."

"Well, let's find out," Ned said, gesturing impatiently at the screen.

The video cut to a waist-up shot of Matt, talking to a reporter.

"Hell, yes," Mason exclaimed, elated to see him being interviewed, being taken seriously. "That's Matt," he told Ned.

He had spiffed up for the camera, with a collared shirt worn under a tweed blazer, and he'd cut his hair again; it was short and tidy. That was definitely intentional—calculated for media appeal, just as wearing the jacket of an archetypal college professor was. The caption at the bottom of the screen read "Matt Rifkin, Cal State LA."

"I've done a comprehensive search for the K94BL molecule," Matt told the reporter, "and I've notified the FDA because the results are so alarming. Not every sample of Billy Blood tested positive for it, but even one positive result is too many. The root of the problem is that the company won't disclose how the product is processed. It happens in China, and without transparency we have no way of knowing how or when this toxin is incorporated."

The reporter asked a couple of soft leading questions, and Matt explained in lay terms what prions actually were, and the potential this one had for causing disease.

Mason was amazed: Matt was calm, and confident, and spoke authoritatively. He was definitely the right scientist to put in front of the camera.

"He's like a different person," he told Ned. "Whenever I've talked to him, he curses like a sailor."

The video returned to the studio newsreader, who said, "That's the word today from a local university. An FDA official subsequently spoke to reporters in Washington," and then cut to a thick guy with a comb-over standing in front of an array of microphones, the agency's logo wallpapering the backdrop. Over his shirt and tie he wore the white jacket of a clinician, complete with his name embroidered in cobalt blue above his pocket. The caption identified him as "Assistant Deputy General Manager—Center for Soft Drink Evaluation and Research."

"Why is he wearing medical garb?" Mason said. "He's a bureaucrat. No way would he be spending time with patients."

"It's an affectation for the cameras," Ned said. "They want you to think 'healer' instead of 'bureaucrat.'"

"The last thing we want to do is interfere with American business," the meta-doctor said, "and we have no mandate or desire to regulate lifestyle products or their ingredients. But if there is any merit to this study out of"—he looked down to consult his notes—"California, we will pass that information along in due course to the appropriate agencies."

"Jesus," Mason scoffed. "Way to come out swinging."

The newsreader appeared again. "In addition to toxic ingredients, Billy Blood has another crisis on its hands," he intoned. "The company is headquartered in Los Angeles, and today the local weekly *Va-Voom* published a sordid tale of marketing ... gone horribly awry."

"This is my thing," Mason said.

The video cut to a reporter standing on the sidewalk in front of the Billy Blood building. There were three news vans visible in the shot, their transmission antennae stretching skyward, and a number of people milling around on the front steps.

"Look at that crowd," Ned said. "Between you and your psychic friend, you certainly got some attention."

Locking eyes with the camera, the reporter explained, "Anonymous sources confirmed to *Va-Voom* that Billy Blood CEO Tyler Frey personally and secretly commissioned the recent attacks on the company's billboards and products—an act that he publicly described as terrorism." She ran the clip they had seen weeks ago of Frey making that allegation, and then explained how Frey had told the vandal the exact wording to use, even the color of paint.

"Santos really did it," Mason said. "It's public knowledge now."

"She didn't mention the shady law firm, though," Ned said. "I wonder how they managed to keep their names out of the story?"

Mason inhaled sharply when the video cut to a few seconds of that painfully familiar footage of him standing amid the salty snacks in Sargasian's store, eyes clenched shut, trying to do psychometry on a six-pack of Billy Blood.

Concern in her eyes, the reporter said, "Frey went so far in the ruse as to hire a purported psychic to uncover the culprit. We reached out to Mr. Wrathway today, but all trace of him has been removed from local listings. The clear implication is that Wrathway colluded with Frey in this cynical charade to market the lifestyle drink."

Mason felt his face turning red. He hit the pause button and said, "So now I'm responsible for this?"

"Wow," Ned said. "The media giveth, and the media taketh away."

"They did not reach out to me," he said angrily. "I can't even defend myself."

"You could, if you're willing to fess up that you're Nelson Wrathway."

Mason thought about that. If the reporter couldn't find him, it meant his anonymity was intact. "I guess I don't want to do that. Maybe I should just let it go."

Ned nodded. "No matter what you do or say, you'll never have any control of how they spin the story. And in a week it won't matter—the media have the attention span of a mayfly."

The reporter continued, "The psychic may have disappeared, but CEO Tyler Frey wasn't so lucky."

The final clip showed Frey, forcing a taut smile, sitting in the backseat of a black town car, swarmed by photographers and video cameras as his driver inched through the mob. When the camera zoomed out, Mason saw they were on the ramp out of the parking lot under the Billy Blood building.

"I'm glad you did this," Ned said when the video ended. "Even if nobody is held accountable, you may have slowed down the demand for goat blood."

"I hope so," Mason said, and squeezed his hand. He was grateful that Ned got it. "I'm going to read Santos's article."

Ned went back to work, and Mason found the story on the *Va-Voom* website. Santos had laid everything out accurately, but like the TV reporter he didn't mention Mangel and Stein. It seemed unlikely that he would have been able to confirm other parts of the story but not their involvement. Regardless, it was gratifying to read it; Santos had pursued the story and set it free in the world.

Mason spent the rest of the day watching national TV coverage of the story, and scanning the news items that popped up online. Matt's story eclipsed Santos's in every report, which suited Mason just fine; it meant less attention was focused on the mysterious Billy Blood psychic, and Frey would have more pressing issues than trying to link Mason to the *Va-Voom* story. Every report that did mention the psychic implied that Mason had been complicit in the con and had mysteriously vanished, but at least none of them had figured out who he actually was. Eventually it became clear that no new details were going to emerge, at least until Frey broke his silence—every news outlet was using Santos's story as their only source material.

Toward dinnertime, Ned moved into the kitchen, working on a pie with some cherries he'd found at the farmers market. When Peggy got home from work, Mason closed his laptop and went inside to greet her. She usually changed out of her formal law-firm attire and let her hair down as soon as she came in, but she had already seen the news.

"Yay, Mason," she said, sliding onto a barstool and pulling the pin out of her hair. "You and Matt took down Billy Blood. The CEO looked like a war criminal, slinking away in his limo."

Mason sat with her. "The timing couldn't have been better, to have both stories break on the same day."

"There are no coincidences, right?" she said. "You two must have psychically synchronized it."

"Maybe they'll ditch the CEO," Ned said. He scooped up the pie and slid it into the oven, then set the timer. "For Billy Blood, the best you can hope for is to temporarily knock a digit or two off their market value."

Mason said, "At least the info is out there. People should know what they're drinking, and how things are being marketed to them. The only thing I don't get is why Santos didn't say anything about Mangel and Stein. There was clear evidence that their guy Valdez arranged the whole thing."

"If Valdez is a lawyer," Peggy said, "the first thing he'd do is weasel out of any responsibility."

She ought to know, Mason thought.

"I bet Valdez made a deal with your journalist," she said, "to keep his name and his firm out of the story in exchange for confirming the rest of it."

"It makes sense," Mason said. "I bet you're right."

Ned scowled. "Everyone in this town is working an angle."

"That's capitalism, baby," Peggy said, and went to change.

Ned set to work on making pesto, loading the food processor with basil, almonds, and garlic.

"Do you need a hand?" Mason asked.

"You can pick the noodles," he said. "I think we have rotini or penne."

Mason picked rotini, and by the time they'd

finished the pasta, Ned's pie had cooled enough to dish up. It was delectable, as always.

After dinner, Mason collected all the notes he'd made about the case and put them into the Billy Blood folder in his drawer. It was satisfying to be done with it and file it away.

"Billy Blood's stock has really tanked overseas," Ned called to him from the living room. "I'll send you an article about it."

Mason opened it on his laptop. It was a stock market update from the *Charlotte Scoop & Analyzer*'s Shanghai bureau. He scanned it quickly; the writer's analysis was that Billy Blood's share price had dropped so precipitously that it might never recover.

"I didn't expect such an extreme reaction," Mason said, carrying his computer out to join Ned on the sofa. It was exactly what Catherine had called the wisdom of the market—bad news had devalued the company.

"It's because of the contamination issue, more than the terrorism thing," Ned said, looking up from his tablet. "Wall Street has no problem with liars and cheats, but they would interpret the prion story as potential financial liability. Even so, I don't think it'll wipe out the corporation."

"Still no word from Frey, it seems."

"You didn't read to the end," Ned said.

Mason went back to the article. Sure enough,

almost as an afterthought, the writer explained that Billy Blood had announced Frey's departure, effective immediately. His severance included a $22 million payout.

"I can't believe he did all that damage," Mason said, "and then they gave him all that freaking money. What's wrong with these people?"

"It sounds like a lot," Ned said, "but in corporate terms it's not, compared to their assets. It's like those people who hang around the gas station and bug you when you're pumping gas. You might be standing there with several hundred bucks in your pocket, so it's no big deal to give them a dollar or two to get them to go away."

"Still, handing someone $22 million doesn't seem like much of a punishment," he said.

Ned shrugged. "Things work differently at that level."

Mason stretched and went out to the balcony to clear his head. He couldn't be resentful about Frey's payout, he decided; he'd done his part to shed light on the truth, and the rest of it was beyond his influence. As he honed his skills and expanded his psychic repertoire, the only thing he could count on was that the path was increasingly unpredictable. It worked, though. He could live with that.

He spent the rest of the evening with Ned, half reading and half watching the movie Ned had gotten into. Not long before bedtime, Mason asked him, "Is there any of that pie left?"

"You know damn well there is," Ned said, and laughed.

Mason walked into the kitchen and found a sheet of paper on the refrigerator door. It was a full-color screen shot taken from that awful video clip of him holding the six-pack in the liquor store. WANTED BY INTERPOL had been added in big block letters. He smiled at Peggy's sense of humor. He looked more closely at the image, hoping that the blotchiness on his face was a printer artifact rather than how his skin really looked. The he sat and had his pie.